# ON TWO FRONTS

Two brothers are torn from each other by the struggle between Orthodox Judaism and the Reform movement in revolutionary nineteenth century Hungary

A NOVEL BY
**Yirmeyahu Bindman**

BASED ON A STORY BY
**Sarah Feldbrand**

P·U·B·L·I·S·H·E·R·S
New York · London · Jerusalem

# ON TWO FRONTS

Copyright © 1990

All rights reserved. This book, or any part thereof, may not be reproduced in any form whatsoever without the express written permission of the copyright holder.

ISBN 1-56062-028-5

Published and distributed
in the U.S., Canada and overseas by
C.I.S. Publishers and Distributors
180 Park Avenue, Lakewood, New Jersey 08701
(201) 905-3000 Fax: (201) 367-6666

Distributed in Israel by
C.I.S. International (Israel)
Rechov Mishkalov 18
Har Nof, Jerusalem
Tel: 02-538-935

Distributed in the U.K. and Europe by
C.I.S. International (U.K.)
1 Palm Court, Queen Elizabeth Walk
London, England N16
Tel: 01-809-3723

Cover design by Ronda Kruger Israel
Book design by Joseph Neumark
Typography by Leah Langleben

*On Two Fronts* describes the turbulent events in Hungary during the latter half of the nineteenth century, both within the Jewish community and in the world around it. It was a time of revolution and social upheaval, and among the Jews, it brought to Hungary the struggle between Orthodox Judaism and the Reform movement. The main characters in this book are fictional. However, some of the characters, such as Laszos Kossuth, are historical, while others, such as Moshe Chaim Sonnenschein, are modelled after recognizable historical figures with similarities intended only in the general sense.

# CHAPTER ONE

Snowflakes whirled about the faces of the young couple as they came up to the door of their house. The path had been cleared that morning, but already it was covered with freshly-fallen snow, trodden down until it crunched beneath their boots. Chaim Eisenstadt knocked on the door, and he and his wife Feige stood waiting, blowing on their hands, smiling to each other at the force of the gale howling around them in the black night.

Feige's mother opened the door, and they stepped straight into the living room, keeping away from the rug while they took off their hats and coats and mufflers. They went up to the fire and stood in front of it, letting the warmth calm them as the tension seeped from their bodies.

It was nearly midnight, with *Chanukah* only a week past. Everyone in the little Hungarian town of Grossverdan was huddled indoors, wrapped in the warmth of their firesides as a shield against the long winter that lay ahead.

"Are the boys asleep?" Feige asked her mother.

"Yes, they are. Not a word from either of them. Not until after a bit of shouting, though."

Feige laughed.

"I didn't suppose it would be any different," she said.

She took off her shawl and sat down at the table, on which lay a few leather-bound books and a piece of paper printed in Yiddish and Hungarian.

"Have you seen this, Mommie?" she asked, holding it up for her to see.

"Yes I have, and it made me feel a little shaky."

Feige drew up her chair and scanned the paper once more. It was a proclamation notice from the *Kehillah* of the town, summarizing an address given by the Rabbi on the previous day when news had arrived of mob attacks on the Jews in the big cities of Budapest and Pressburg. He had called for fasting, prayer and repentance to nullify the evil decree.

It was no secret to anyone that great events were afoot in Hungary, that days of destiny were at hand. Nearly sixty years had passed since the French Revolution had begun the overthrow of the old monarchies of Europe, after which the French armies under Napoleon had reached Hungary and even tried to conquer Russia. The ultimate French defeat had only intensified the pressure for change and reform.

In the wake of the French defeat, the Hapsburg dynasty, ancient rulers of Austria, was again set up on the throne to manage an Empire of over fifty million people differing widely in language and outlook. Of these minorities Hungary was the senior. Its aristocracy was undefeated by the German-speaking Austrians and its rising middle class was eager for expansion and opportunity, each section of society jealous of the other. The Emperor Ferdinand in Vienna was unable to control this situation, and in his inadequacy, he tried to reunite the warring factions of his Empire with their common hatred of the Jews. Each segment of the society saw in the Jews either an enemy or a traitor. And it was not long before their verbal violence

ON·TWO·FRONTS

spilled over into the streets.

By contrast, the Hungarian liberals were attempting to modernize the country socially and economically, to sweep away the moral corruption of the Aristocratic Era. As Hungarian nationalists, they campaigned for the adoption of the Hungarian language in the country, and since most Jews did not speak Hungarian, their position in a future national culture was an important issue. Thus it was that the Jews were threatened from all sides. And now, in 1848, the radicals under the leadership of Laszos Kossuth, determined to bring matters to decision, had taken up the clarion-call of reform.

The feeling in the air was of youth, vital and unrestrained. "Bliss was it in that dawn to be alive," was the contemporary poetic phrase that described the mood, "but to be young was very heaven."

Chaim and Feige Eisenstadt had been born into a Jewish world of authority and responsibility, but even they were affected by the emotional outpouring they sensed all around them. As they prepared for sleep on this winter night beside their two young sons Elya and Menachem, they thought of their hopes for the future, suddenly so uncertain and dangerous, yet also holding its promise of opportunity and renewal.

Events began to move swiftly. In February of 1848, the population of Paris rose against King Louis Philippe, who had been placed on the throne in order to preserve Monarchy and Liberty together; the task was of course impossible, and when the mind of the British government began to move towards increasing democracy on the Continent they withdrew their support from him. He and his family fled the country, casting themselves as helpless refugees at the feet of Queen Victoria, and France became once more a Republic.

The revolutionary trend spread out like a grass fire. Talk of equality was everywhere. Every country in Europe had its own revolution, even Switzerland, and the world watched as Hapsburg Austria came under pressure, with clashes in Vienna between the troops and student demonstrators pressing for a constitution.

The Eisenstadts at their country fireside knew most of this, not because they read the newspapers, but because talk of these questions was on everyone's lips. They and thousands like them were being drawn into events where mass opinions were what counted, and the names of the spokesmen for those opinions were becoming known from end to end of the land.

Of these spokesmen none was more significant than Laszos Kossuth, a man apparently born to arouse passions and to lead them on the march. As a young lawyer he had instinctively been drawn to politics, and he obtained for himself a position as a reporter on the proceedings of the Budapest parliament, the Diet. Soon, he became the editor of the *Pesti Hirlap* newspaper, and from this position he made himself into the premier advocate of reform in the country. Eloquent and fiery articles poured from his pen, and his wide knowledge and critical faculties, combined with a commanding appearance in public, eventually brought about his election to the Diet as a member in his own right.

As the Austrian uprising began to spread, he rose in the assembly to deliver a daring speech of extraordinary power. He demanded the removal of the Viennese monarchy as the only way to secure the liberties of Hungary, and amid scenes of panic among the courtiers, the Emperor Ferdinand recognized his declaration of independence. And thus, Hungary became a republic, with a program of civil liberties for all.

These were the winds blowing through the Jewish towns such as Grossverdan. The fate of nations was being decided on the streets, and homes became warmer and more precious as outside conditions grew steadily more disruptive. The Jews looked into the Torah, but they also began to wonder what advantages might be opened to them if their legal segregation in the ghetto proved to be impermanent.

Was continued segregation the only way in which the Torah could be preserved? Or was it only a remnant of the Middle Ages, standing in the way of their natural dignity? Which sane person would choose to retain degradation, assuming it was not still more degrading to be on an equal footing with the other nations? They did not know. All they could be sure of was that their fate was not to be of their own making. Their status was in the hands of the Almighty, now as always, and it was for them only to pass the tests He might choose to set for them.

# CHAPTER TWO

The years had been increasingly kind to Laszos Kossuth. His newspaper was in every hand, and his strikingly handsome figure was present wherever opinions were in the making. He had fame and power, he was both loved and respected, and his only disappointment was that he and his wife still had no child of their own. He worked extremely hard, but still, his work was not toil; it rose up from deep within him like a wellspring, and his ability lay in directing and controlling it. Some called him a genius, and indeed, the use of that word indicated well what he meant to accomplish. It was the title of a hero, a climber of mountains, a victor over enemies, but the wise might have smiled a little as he passed across the scene and murmured, "One who overcomes his inclination is greater than one who conquers a city."

But for the moment he was the kingpin of the country, the

"mover and shaker." Temporarily leaving Budapest, he threw himself into a whirlwind tour of the provinces to gather support, paying attention everywhere to the task of influencing Jewish opinion as the key to his success. He knew that if he could reassure the Jews themselves as to their safety he could more easily turn to the pacification of the country as a whole.

Everyone wanted to hear the man whose energy and determination held so much promise for them, and he was anxious to convey his good sense and reliability. When he came to Grossverdan, both Jews and gentiles turned out to watch as the set of carriages with their prancing horses came bouncing towards them in the spring sunshine. Respectful, but slightly uneasy, they stood at the sides of the road as he disembarked and shook hands with the dignitaries who had assembled to greet him. There was a reception at the town hall, and afterwards he spoke in the synagogue to an audience less overawed by him than most but somewhat more anxious to hear what he had to say.

He smiled in greeting as he mounted the pulpit.

"My fellow citizens," he began. "Though your ancestors have long lived among us in Hungary, I am still among the first to address you by this title. Yet I do not mean to imply that your lives here until now have been barren of achievement. On the contrary, all of us have come to set great store by your kindness and refinement, as well as your energy and enterprise, and therefore it is none too soon that I come to address you as brothers.

"All across the world the peoples are rising to assert the Brotherhood of Man. We want no more of division and restriction, of the laws that have separated us since all our countries were founded. In America, an entirely new nation has arisen, based on principles of freedom from its very foundation; all our hearts turn towards them as an example of how the affairs of state should be run. Among them, the Jews have never suffered discrimination; they are able to make their way in society exactly as they please. We, too, see the definition of Jewish identity in legal terms as a restriction of the spirit."

Glances were exchanged in the audience. Who knew where this might end? But the eyes of Kossuth were gazing into the distance. He continued to speak of the future, of the tasks ahead, of the progress being brought to every locality by the development of the railway train. His listeners nodded silently. They knew about the railway train. They realized that what he said would indeed come to pass, and they were calmed by his straightforwardness and sincerity.

Chaim Eisenstadt and his father-in-law strolled out into the street at the end with the rest of the audience. Most dispersed to their homes, but some lingered in conversation outside, watching as the reformer strode over to his carriage in the gathering dusk. Chaim turned to the older man.

"I don't suppose it'll do too much harm, do you?" he remarked.

His father-in-law smiled indulgently. "Oh, they'll make changes all right, and good ones, too, but I don't really set too much store by these coffee house philosophers. Plenty of things can happen in the world of which they take no account, and in the end, the truth will still be the same. Anyway, we can't have the fellow make us late for *Minchah*, can we now?"

He looked around the group, asking with his eyes the question that was asked every afternoon, and he nodded in satisfaction as he reckoned up the answers to the number of a *minyan*. The suite of carriages had already left on their journey, and with a gesture he beckoned to the group to enter for the prayer.

For the reformers, that summer was the time of high noon. The Austrian premier Metternich, who had so long served the cause of conservatism with his unique diplomatic skill, had been forced from power. Budapest was now a capital city, lively with debate and celebration, attracting immigrants from all over Hungary to its new commercial and personal opportunities. Chaim and Feige, too, decided to seek out the new horizons; they took a small apartment in the older Buda section of the city, and there they settled in with their two boys, a little bewildered by the bustle and commotion around them.

The city had a singular beauty. Draped over the hills on the banks of the River Danube, it retained a touch of the Oriental atmosphere that dated from its occupation by the Turks. The Jewish community contained many *Sephardim* whose families had arrived during that time. Chaim obtained a job working in a private library kept by a wealthy pious Jew in his mansion, and thus he was able to keep up his learning and even enter areas of thought he had not known before.

It was, however, not to be considered that this heavenly freedom would last forever. Whole classes of the old society were still in existence, still wealthy, and unprepared to let the reins of power slip from their grasp. Rumors began to spread through the new capital that a counterattack was being planned in Vienna, and soon they were confirmed. In December, the Emperor Ferdinand was replaced by his nephew Franz Josef, who issued a decree declaring the concessions made to Kossuth as null and void. Thus the whole of Hungary was considered to be in a state of rebellion, and an army was sent to invade it and return it to the law.

The people of Hungary were immediately mobilized into a revolutionary militia to defend the country, and despite the pogroms that had only recently ended, many Jews volunteered for service. They insisted on being sent to the front and performed many heroic deeds in the service of the new order. Much of this was a tribute to the abilities of Kossuth and to the goodwill he had succeeded in arousing. At first, the fighting went well for the Hungarians, especially after further revolutionary disturbances broke out in Vienna itself, but then came disaster. The Russian Tsar Nicholas I mobilized his huge army to help his fellow sovereign and invaded Hungary from the north.

Both of these armies laid siege to Budapest. No effective government functioned in the city, and while the militiamen made frantic efforts to defend it street by street, a state of chaos descended on the civilian population. The Eisenstadt family remained sheltered in their apartment for as long as they could, *davening* and saying *Tehillim*. Occasionally, they spoke together in low tones, cradling the children in their arms.

"What do you think will be happening in Grossverdan?" Feige asked her husband.

"I think the Russians will have taken it without a fight," Chaim replied. "Everyone should be safe. There is no reason for them to pay any attention to it, except to take food for themselves and the horses."

"Well I hope they don't start plundering my parents," said Feige.

"Don't worry. They're probably thinking more about how we might be faring than about their troubles."

And thus the hours lengthened into days. They baked flour into a kind of flat bread like *matzos* on a wood-burning stove. Occasionally, they were startled by the sound of shots or a shell burst from the streets outside, but there was no way of knowing what was happening in general. Thousands of proclamation leaflets had been printed exhorting the population to remain calm, but no real news filtered through.

On the third day of the siege, Menachem Eisenstadt suddenly fell ill with a sickness that neither of his parents had ever seen before; they had no idea of what it might be, and they were terribly afraid because they knew the risk of epidemics in wartime. In their extremity, they discussed what might be best to do for him.

"I'll have to take him to some kind of hospital," Chaim said.

"There's no way to be sure you could reach the place," said Feige. "And besides, what would they give him there?"

"Unless we know what it is we can't even give him proper nursing," Chaim insisted. "We can't just keep him here by ourselves."

They bundled him up in blankets against the cold, and Chaim carried him out, half walking, half running through the narrow alleyways, keeping as close as possible to the side of the street. He knew there was a small charitable hospital about two miles away. When he reached it he was not surprised to find it had been turned into a casualty station and was overflowing with wounded. Overcome with dismay, he sat down on a bench to rally his spirits. Soon, he saw a young doctor come out and turn towards him.

The doctor looked as if he had not slept for days. Red-eyed and haggard, he asked Chaim what was the matter. He picked up Menachem and examined him blearily, amid the pitiful sound of cries and groans from the sick and wounded.

"He has scarlet fever," he announced. "Take him home and put him to bed, and give him as much water as he will drink. And if he gets out of it alive he'll be just as lucky as the rest of us."

Chaim nodded silently in reply.

"Thank you, sir," he said. "Thank you for your attention."

He took back the child and shuffled over to the bench to rest for a few minutes before setting out on the journey back home. His mind was barely functioning, what with food running out, a sick child, the risk of further infection and enemy forces poised to enter the city. How was it all going to end? He closed his eyes for a moment, breathing steadily to try to marshal his thoughts.

Suddenly, he heard a faint whistling sound from above. He opened his eyes and looked around him, feeling a stir of alarm as it grew louder. Other people had heard it too, and a noisy commotion began to break out in the corridors. There was running and shouting.

"Down!" a voice bellowed out above the din. "Everybody get down!"

Chaim threw himself to the floor, dragging the child with him, just before a terrible crash shook the entire building. A giant mortar shell had exploded in a direct hit. The roof of the hospital was destroyed entirely, rubble was falling all around, and a choking dust filled the air. For a minute, there was deathly silence, then voices were heard crying out for help. The staff began combing through the wreckage looking for survivors, while volunteers came running to the scene.

The doctor who had examined Menachem found two nurses still on duty in his ward.

"Wilma, see what you can find on that side," he said. "Magda, come with me."

Together the nurse and the doctor searched through the half-wrecked passages, until suddenly the sound of a child's faint cry came to Magda's ears. She went over to investigate, feeling a sharp pang at the thought of an infant suffering in this disaster. And there she found the child, lying swathed in a blanket next to an unconscious man on the floor. She bent down and touched the man on the shoulder, but he did not stir. She picked up the child, peering tenderly into his face.

"About fifteen months old," she murmured to herself.

The doctor saw her and came over.

"That's the child I just examined," he said. "What happened to the father?"

She pointed down. "This must be him. He's dead."

"There's no time to bother with him now," said the doctor. "I'll take care of the body after we've tended to all the survivors."

He went down the corridor, shouting for assistance as the rescuers began to arrive from outside. Magda took the child and put him down in a corner. She looked at him more steadily and spoke to him.

### ON·TWO·FRONTS

"You are ill, my little one," she whispered. "And your father's dead. But don't worry. G-d has sent you to me, to keep you safe and console me in my loneliness."

# CHAPTER THREE

The first thing Chaim saw after the explosion was a thick red mist that seemed to be floating before his eyes. There was a roaring sound in his ears, and a groan escaped his lips as he tried to sit up and failed. He must have fainted again, because the next time he opened his eyes he was propped against the wall and a man was offering him a cup of water. He sipped at it and lay still for a few seconds, feeling the void of unconsciousness slipping away from him, and the mobility returning to his stiffened limbs.

"Where am I?" he asked the man, his voice croaking.

"You are all right now, my friend," grinned his helper. "This is the hospital, or at any rate it used to be."

"Hospital?" He put his hand confusedly to his head, trying to pierce through the fog in his thoughts, and then he came awake with a start as he remembered.

"My son! Where is my son?"

"I didn't see a child here," replied the man anxiously. "You were alone when I found you."

Chaim made a supreme effort and struggled to his feet, staring around distractedly.

"I must find my son!" he cried.

"Hey, hey, you're not going anywhere in a state like that!" said the rescuer, taking hold of him by the shoulders.

Chaim swayed as he tried to fend off the gentle restraint.

"You're going to have to sit quietly for a while, and then you can go and look for your son," the man continued. "Don't worry, he won't be far away."

And so Chaim sat down and drank a little more water. Then he dragged himself to his feet once more and began to search through the grime and chaos around him. He went into every room, looking in every corner, gritting his teeth against the dizziness and nausea that threatened to overwhelm him. The place was full of people, staff, patients, rescuers and officials, and relatives searching for their loved ones. The stench of death and destruction was everywhere, filling the nostrils, yet he saw people working with tireless courage to save the lives of survivors and bring them out to safety. He saw scenes of grief, and he also saw joyous reunions as families emerged from the hour of danger.

But there was no such joy for him. After an hour of investigation, he found no trace of Menachem. Even more than his own desperate anguish he knew that he would now have to tell Feige that an unknown fate had befallen their son.

He trailed back home miserably, expecting his wife to be distraught when she heard the news, but to his surprise she only pressed her hands together in her lap and bowed her head.

"I know that he is alive," she said quietly. "I know that Hashem is caring for him."

Thus silently, they bent themselves to wait out the emergency, caring for Elya as a kind of surety against his brother's return, for it was not yet certain what the outcome would be for any of them.

The events of the conflict were now showing the Hungarian leaders just how fragile their experiment in democracy had been.

## ON·TWO·FRONTS

Kossuth was not a military man, but as soon as the two invading armies crossed the frontier he had gone immediately to the front to take overall charge of resistance. He was not encouraged by what he saw, and after exhorting the militia commanders to resist as strongly as possible, without wasting their efforts in hopeless positions, he returned to Budapest in the hope that his presence there would serve as a rallying point for the city's population.

Upon arriving in the city, he first drove to his home, hoping for a respite of an hour or so from the pressures of the campaign. Covered in mud and dust from the journey, he went inside and began wearily to take off his cloak and boots with the help of his valet. He paused a moment to catch his breath, and as he stood there in his stockinged feet, he was astonished to hear from within the house, faint but piercing, the unmistakable sound of a baby's cry.

Barely able to believe his ears, he strode up the stairs and into the bedroom, from where the sound was coming.

"Magda? Magda?" he called out. "Is that you?"

His wife was standing at the foot of the bed as he came in, and she turned hastily to face him, her eyes wide. On the bed before her lay a baby boy. They stood facing one another uneasily for a few seconds before Magda plucked up the courage to speak.

"Hello, Laszos," she said lamely.

Kossuth worked his lips to free them from the grime of the road.

"What have you got there?" he asked.

She smiled. "It's a baby."

"I can see it's a baby," her husband retorted. "But whose baby is it?"

Magda clasped her hands in front of her and looked down at the floor.

"His father was killed when a shell hit the hospital," she murmured. "The baby is ill. I brought him here to take care of him. Oh, Laszos!" she burst out. "Can't I take care of him?"

Kossuth stood silently, trying to work out where he was and what to do. It wasn't every day that one came back home from a battlefront to find oneself an adoptive father. And how could he ever hope to trace the mother of this unknown foundling in a war-torn city? Surely, it would be unthinkable to refuse him this one chance of survival in a proper home. He nodded in assent.

"I suppose it will be all right," he said. "But what if we have a child of our own?"

His wife gave him a radiant smile.

"Then they'll be brothers! Don't worry, he'll be no trouble at all."

And thus, while independent Hungary hovered on the brink of defeat, little Menachem Eisenstadt received the best of attention in the strange house where he had been brought. He recovered from his fever and began to smile at the man and the woman who had relieved his pain. They in their turn began to feel happy and proud that they had saved his life, and it was not long before they began to look upon him with particular feelings of affection. He was their consolation in the hour of trouble, the center and symbol of their hopes for a better future.

One of the last acts of Kossuth's government before it fell to the invaders was to declare equal rights for all Jews within its territory. A clear break was made with the ghetto past, and though the reactionary monarch reimposed the previous order when his army took control of the city, it was impossible for the position to remain as it had been. As peace returned to the troubled Empire, it was clear to everyone that the Emperor himself must introduce liberal laws in order to manage the rapid current of change in all areas of the life of the country.

The government in Vienna soon conceded equality to Hungary, and changed the name of the monarchy to the Austro-Hungarian Empire. Budapest remained a secondary capital city, still seething with its race and class hostilities and its anti-Semitism, but calmed by the return of prosperity and the gradual tide of progress that marked the Victorian Era all over the world.

Kossuth resumed his public activities, though now in the company of other notable figures, writing and speaking with increasing assurance as the ideas of the time began to flow once more in his direction. In spite of himself, he was happy to have the foundling child in his household. Before the invasion, all his fiery energy had gone into his political campaigning, but after the struggle was over he was more than grateful to have the child's affection.

Menachem became very fond of Kossuth, gazing up at him wide-eyed as he sat in the big chair at the head of the table, sitting on the floor while he held meetings with his associates, watching him at his desk hour after hour. Magda tended to spoil him a little with food and treats, openly regarding him as a gift from heaven, yet always apprehensive of the day when he would ask her his origins and she would have to tell him the truth.

Once the war was over, Chaim and Feige decided to remain in Budapest, desperately clinging to the hope of being reunited with Menachem. Feige continued to believe and affirm that he was safe, and Chaim would do nothing to cross her motherly intuition. He himself was not so sure of the matter, yet he also could not help feeling that some manifestation of Providence was in progress, and in his prayers he constantly begged for divine help in fulfilling it. He kept his library position, and in his spare time, he wandered about the city, half-searching for his son and gaining a knowledge that might somehow help him if any clue came to hand.

A year passed, then another, and a third. By now Chaim had begun to speak a little Hungarian. He got into the habit of chatting for a few minutes with the newspaper vendor who stood outside the door of their building, to be neighborly and to keep up the language. During one such conversation the man was rambling about some scandal in political circles in the city, and Chaim was listening to him with only half an ear.

"And what about Kossuth, then?" he heard the vendor say. "That child of his? A friend of my wife's was in there talking to the maid, and she said she saw the boy was circumcised."

He raised a bushy eyebrow in waggish humor at his friend, puffing gently on his pipe as he savored the piquant situation. Chaim's eyes opened wide; the whole street seemed to be swimming around him. He stared at the vendor for a moment.

"Yes, yes," he stammered. "I have to be on my way."

He walked on unsteadily, hardly even sure of the direction in which he was going, trying to separate the thoughts that jumbled together in his mind.

"Could it be? The age would be just about right. And even if it's another Jew I'll have to find out and redeem him."

He decided to go straight to the Kossuth house without arousing his wife's hopes beforehand, and so half an hour later, with his heart in his mouth, he stood knocking on the door of the reformer.

A maid opened it, and asked him his business.

ON·TWO·FRONTS

"I must speak to Mr. Kossuth in person."

The maid eyed him doubtfully.

"Please wait here," she said.

Chaim stood on the spot listening to the exchange of voices from within as Kossuth was told of the visitor. The reformer worried to some extent about his personal safety, but his usual approach was to set such considerations aside and receive visitors freely, so he asked for Chaim to be brought in. Still, Kossuth was a little disconcerted at the unhappy figure, hatted and bearded, who entered and stood before him, refusing the offer of a chair.

"What can I do for you, good sir?"

Chaim hesitated, and then took a deep breath.

"I have not come to speak to you officially, but on a different matter entirely," he began. "It has come to my attention that . . . the child in your house is of Jewish origin."

Kossuth turned in his seat and looked up at him, thunderstruck. He eyed him keenly, but Chaim bore up under the glance.

"Therefore it is my duty to ask you how he came to be here," he continued.

There was silence in the room. Kossuth frowned and bowed his head for a moment in thought, and then he looked up again, his expression serious and grave.

"May I ask your interest in the matter?"

"I am interested in the welfare of the children of our people, and besides. . . I was parted from my own son three years ago, during the invasion."

Kossuth's mouth tightened for a moment, and then he nodded curtly.

"Yes, I see. Wait here for a moment."

He got up, went out and strode over to the foot of the stairs.

"Magda?" he called up. "Magda!"

His wife came out to the landing with a smile and leaned over the banister.

"Yes, Laszos?"

Then she saw his face, and she knew something serious had occurred. She came quickly down the stairs and went up to him.

"What is it?"

He leaned on the banister.

"A Jewish man has come who says he was parted from his baby son in the invasion," he whispered quickly and gently into her ear.

She stared into his eyes, her face pale.

"What do you mean?"

He spread his hands despairingly.

"Didn't we know the boy was Jewish? What can we say? We are not aristocrats who take whatever they want."

All the breath seemed to flow out of Magda, and even her husband was startled by the volume of the tears that burst from within her as she collapsed in weeping against the rail. He patted her gently on the shoulder until she was done.

"Come now," he said. "Let us go in and hear his story, and we will decide what the answer should be."

# CHAPTER FOUR

At first, the reunited Eisenstadt family had great difficulty finding its balance again. Elya was none too pleased to be sharing his home with a brother of whose existence he had never known. The children sulked and squabbled, and it took all the efforts of the parents to prevent an open rift from developing. For Menachem the transition had been very abrupt, and he often spoke of Laszos and Magda Kossuth and the things they had said and done. He seemed to consider them in all respects as equal to his real family, and even to accord them a kind of superiority. For a time, the family spoke in Hungarian as well as Yiddish to help him acclimatize, but it was an uphill struggle all the way, and Feige often voiced feelings near to heartbreak over the possibility that he might have been deeply affected.

Eventually, they decided that Budapest itself would never provide the setting for a reconciliation. They returned and there things began to go more smoothly. The two boys would explore the new surroundings together, and Menachem became accustomed to Yiddish as Elya chatted to him and told him the things he was learning and drew him into the circle of the extended family. The two brothers became quite close, and by the time they reached the age of *chinuch* they were very attached to each other, intrigued at the circumstances that had drawn them in such different directions so early in their lives.

Elya was calmer, more assured, more at ease with the world and his own place in it, while Menachem was interested in relationships between people and within the world as a whole. They began to learn Torah, Elya embracing the outlook of the Jew in its totality with the same assurance, and Menachem always examining each concept by itself to be sure where it fitted into the larger scheme.

Their *Bar-Mitzvahs* came and went, celebrated in the quiet intimacy of the small town. Soon they were in their teens, sedate young boys well thought of by the citizens, advancing steadily in knowledge. It was already time to think of the future, of the wider opportunities the world of learning had to offer.

Years passed and the day finally came when Chaim and Feige sat down together to discuss where to send their sons. After an hour they chose the famous Pressburg *yeshivah*, the chief institution of the Oberland, in the hope that the Ksav Sofer would see fit to enroll the boys under his care.

Pressburg lay near the Danube River as it flowed from Vienna to Budapest, nearer to Vienna but still easily reached from any part of the flatlands of Hungary. It had been an important place on the river for many centuries, once capital of all of Hungary, and always a metropolis for Jews. Only a generation had passed since the Chasam Sofer had established his *yeshivah* there, at the center of the large community, a source of Torah comparable with those in Krakow or Prague. By the time Chaim and Feige left the *Shabbos* candles to flicker out in the darkness they had made their plans; Elya and Menachem would present themselves at the Pressburg *yeshivah* as soon as *Sukkos* was over.

And so, on a crisp autumn morning, the two boys packed their few belongings together and kissed their parents goodbye before clambering into the stagecoach that was to take them to Budapest. There they boarded a paddle-steamer to go up the river to Pressburg, or Bratislava as the Slovakian deck hand called it when they told him their destination. They sat together wrapped up in their coats high on the foredeck to watch the view as they passed slowly through the hills surrounding the city; Esztergom came, and then Komarno, and soon they were steaming by an endlessly flat cultivated plain towards a pass through a line of hills, at whose gate stood the city of Pressburg.

The city was some distance from the river landing, and they were compelled to walk all the way carrying their bags in their hands. Exhausted, they entered the winding streets and asked for directions to the Jewish quarter. Darkness had fallen when they found their way to the *yeshivah*, but when they stumbled through the door, they forgot their tiredness as they gazed around them at the lofty hall. It was filled with dim light from the hanging lamps and with the soft murmur of study as *talmidim* sat swaying over their books in the twilight.

A young man came over to greet them, and he immediately took them to speak to the *Rosh Yeshivah*, the Ksav Sofer, who was sitting engrossed in a *sugya* with his back to the east wall. Rabbi Shmuel Binyamin Sofer shook their hands warmly, asked where they had come from and read the letter of introduction Elya handed him. There and then, he welcomed them to the *yeshivah*, and he told them to bring their bags to his own house for the night until proper lodgings could be found for them.

That night they went to sleep secure in the knowledge that they had begun their *yeshivah* lives under his personal protection, because they had clearly seen that he was a man of immense strength of character. His *shiur* to the whole *yeshivah* would last for three hours, and in the course of it he succeeded in infusing a group of five hundred *talmidim* with a sense of unity and common purpose.

The next morning, after *Shacharis*, he called Elya and Menachem over and introduced them to Reb Shimon Blau, an assistant *mashgiach* who would guide their studies. The first priority was to find suitable partners in learning; after some discussion on this point the *mashgiach* went back to the *Rosh Yeshivah*, and soon returned with his recommendations.

"For you," he said, pointing to Elya, "we have chosen Moshe Chaim Sonnenschein, and you will soon find out what that name means. I can tell you from the start that any time you spend with him will be time well spent. And for you," he told Menachem, "we choose Moshe Greenfeld, and he is also someone well worth listening to, you can be sure."

At first, the boys were not sure how all this came about but they decided their letter of introduction must have had something to do with it. Already they felt the stirring of spiritual growth within them at the prospect of dialogue with these great minds.

So indeed it proved to be. As the learning spread itself out over the days and nights Menachem began to marvel at the depth of Moshe Greenfeld's logical comprehension. His partner had the ability to hold up the *Gemara* like a mirror, revealing to Menachem both the shortcomings and the potential of his understanding. The impression made on him was so deep that at times he even tended to withdraw into himself defensively.

Their temperamental differences led to a certain amount of friction. Menachem was a philosopher who searched for relevance in every topic, while Moshe was a collector of insights, always adding to the tower of his knowledge. Though men may virtually come to blows when they argue over the Torah, they do not part until it has made them into fast friends, and soon even Moshe found that Menachem's questioning could enlarge his own horizons significantly. However, Menachem's level of concentration still did not match that of his partner, and he began to feel uneasy in the assurance of the students all around him.

Elya had come to Pressburg as the acknowledged prodigy of his small-town school. In the larger environment he no longer felt such an easy superiority, and he began to work with diligence. He was vitally aided by Moshe Chaim Sonnenschein, by force of example, for the sterling character of young Moshe Chaim had made an overwhelming impression on him from the very outset. Elya's fund of stories concerning his partner began to grow, beginning with *chessed* and devotion and soon extending to providential occurrences, which held within them a thread of miraculous deliverance. So absorbed did he become in his studies and in his exalted relationship that he tended to lose contact with his brother and to live exclusively in his own world of ambition and fulfillment.

The *yeshivah* was at this time also witnessing the youthful days of other great figures, such as Reb Koppel Reich, later Chief Rabbi of Budapest, and Reb Yehudah Greenwald, who brought glory to the community of Satmar. Their lives were all attended by a good deal of physical hardship; the sleeping accommodations were poor, scattered around the city in different lodging houses and private homes. The fiercely cold Central European winter compelled them to exercise their minds towards keeping warm, as well as in more spiritual directions. Some of the boys tried collecting bricks from a demolished house on a nearby street to heat over a small fire and place under their feet for a little warmth until they cooled. They even poured water around the window-frames and cracks so that it would freeze, because the ice sealed out the wind and made a good insulation.

Under the system known as *kest*, a householder would invite a *talmid* once a week to dine at his table, but there were often not enough of these offers to go round, and the less communicative boys would be left without anyone to take them in. Menachem in particular found the hardships he saw around him upsetting, and he found himself thinking more and more on how he might devise some means of bettering the lot of his brethren.

One evening, soon after the sun had set on a short winter day, he went out walking alone down towards the river bank to ease the tensions in his heart and mind. Kicking at the snow as he went, he allowed his thoughts to roam freely, tumbling over one another in a kind of sober joy. The beauty of the frosty moonlit scene, the urge to know and understand the Torah, and the hopes and frustrations of the whole world as they appeared to him, all seemed to gather strength from each other in a strange onrushing rapture, like the waves of the sea. He felt he had within himself the ability to change things, to give birth to a new order of society with none of the muddle and irrationality of the past, where clarity and sensibility would reign supreme.

"People have to be together," he mused. "They have to realize that they need each other. How can the vital needs of society be left to the individual chance and discretion? Boys in this *yeshivah* are going without food to eat because no one has paid any attention to their requirements."

He stood for a moment on the spot as his thoughts revolved, and a sudden illumination came to him, so startling that he stamped his foot impatiently on the snow.

"I've got it!" he whispered to himself. "We shall ask all the householders to make regular donations to a central cafeteria instead of bringing people into their own homes. That way, all the *talmidim* will be fed!"

He turned back towards the town and strode off, gathering speed as his thoughts began to race.

"Of course they won't go for it so easily, with the weight of tradition as it is. And even if some set an example it won't work unless there is a way of making it public, so that they will know where to go when they decide to go ahead with it. Yes, that's it! A kind of newspaper! It can start with this, and then maybe it will serve for other necessary purposes as well. What an idea! There has never been such a thing before. It would be like unifying what was previously separated, just like at Mount Sinai!"

As he walked along, he began to feel hot inside his coat from the exertion and the excitement within him, so much so that he took off his scarf and let it dangle from his hand as the cold air played about his neck. He would have a place in all this, a role in life. He would be an editor, the chief contributor and judge of the contributions of others, living a life of action close to the workings of destiny. As he came breathlessly into the *Bais Medrash*, he looked quickly around, and he recognized his brother's head from behind. He went over to him, and Elya smiled wearily back as he raised his eyes from the *Gemara*. His eyebrows went up as he saw his brother's sparkling countenance.

"Your cheeks are all rosy," he said. "Where have you been?"

Menachem was too excited to sit down.

"I went for a walk towards the river," he answered, "and I had the most wonderful idea!" He flung his arms wide and grinned broadly.

"If you say so yourself!" Elya laughed. "What's going to save the world, then?"

Menachem told him of his inspiration, emphasizing his words with a raised forefinger. Elya listened, his eyes never leaving his brother's face, nodding to himself as he realized the significance of what he was hearing. Finally Menachem finished, a little out of breath, and waited for the reaction.

"Well, you're talking about big things, aren't you?" said Elya carefully. "If you're going to start something like that you'll have to go into it properly, with care and forethought, because you will have the power to influence people. You will be creating a whole new set of relationships, and I wish you a lot of success, because I think you have the talent to do it."

Menachem beamed with pleasure.

"But you can't possibly attempt such a thing on your own," his brother continued. "You will need someone to help you, maybe even another two people. You'll have to know how to talk to the printers, and of course there is the question of money. Why don't you ask your *chavrusa* what he thinks?"

"I'll surely do that!" cried Menachem. "Thank you, Elya, thank you! And I'll put you down for the very first copy!"

Almost dancing, he turned and made his way to the door. His brother watched him as he went, and when the door had closed he sighed for a moment and rested his head on his hand. Everything around his world of study was changing; the *yeshivah* itself was changing, even his own brother was changing. Or maybe he had been different all along? He shuddered at his memory of the events that had separated Menachem from his family and the Jewish people, and he knew that those events were still proceeding on their disruptive course. Yet what could one say to a sincere young Jew who wanted freedom of expression, freedom of movement? Surely the Almighty would give Menachem the opportunity to realize himself and his ideals. Surely, He would guard the path of the innocent and keep the door closed in the face of one whose wish was not to sin.

# CHAPTER FIVE

The next morning Menachem went to Reb Shimon Blau, the assistant *mashgiach*, and laid the proposals before him. Reb Shimon listened very intently, without showing any reaction at all, and then he remained silent for a full minute. Menachem watched very closely. He saw the lips of Reb Shimon moving softly in prayer, and his head bowed in deep concentration. At last, he raised his face and gave his reply.

"Go forward in the fear of Heaven, and then all will be well."

Menachem was not quite sure what to make of this. It almost seemed like cold water poured on his enthusiasm, and he wondered what doubt there might be in the Reb Shimon's mind. But still, it was a blessing of sorts, and nothing had been said as a direct admonition; and after all, what else could a *mashgiach* be expected to say? He thanked Reb Shimon and then asked how he should go about arranging the finances, in the hope that this might be what had prompted the *mashgiach's* concern. He was given the name of a prominent townsman to approach for a donation, and so it was with relief that he went off to knock on that welcoming door.

With the money in his pocket, he really began to feel like a man of action. His inquiries soon led him to two younger *bachurim* who were eager to join him in the enterprise, and they set about their work with enthusiasm. At the end of the day, after they had finished their *yeshivah* studies, they stayed up late into the night in argument and discussion, writing and rewriting their articles. During the day, they spent all their free time together. In the afternoon, they would go for walks together, picking up where they had left off the night before. A strong bond was forged between the three of them as they worked and exchanged ideas, a bond of the kind that can only develop when friends argue and differ with all their conviction and make up just as enthusiastically.

The first issue was a great success. Not only did the idea of communal dining gather support but an entire dormant spirit of togetherness was reawakened in the community. Menachem's life had undergone a complete change, and his *chavrusa* Moshe was the first to notice the results. There were no more disconsolate sighs, only thoughtful hmm's and satisfied ah's. His turbulent nature seemed to have come closer to contentment than at any time since his arrival in Pressburg. On occasion, he learned with great intensity, his jubilant *Gemara niggun* reverberating through the *Bais Medrash*. At other times, his body continued to sway, but his clouded eyes showed that his mind was elsewhere.

The month of *Shevat* arrived, and the temperatures in the city sank to their lowest level of the whole winter. But Elya was unmindful of the cold; he was hibernating in the *Gemara*, engrossed in the topics, his mind penetrating rapidly to the meaning of each concept and assessing it in manageable terms. He gulped down new knowledge insatiably, delighting in the growth of his process of comprehension, and his greatest happiness was when a difficult point finally became clear. In the late evenings, he would turn to *Midrashic* writings as a relief from the arduous toil of the *Gemara*, and even as he went to sleep his mind continued to travel along the pathways of the day. The Ksav Sofer himself had helped him set up a detailed study schedule in order to cover as many areas as possible in the available time. He seldom saw his brother, and though he was aware that the newsletter had been well received, he had no knowledge of the path Menachem was following.

Had he been aware of the change in his brother's direction, he would have left his idyll with great haste and concern. One of Menachem's collaborators had taken to picking up newspapers and pamphlets in the town in order to scan them for journalistic ideas, and he passed them on to Menachem for his opinions. Menachem had begun to follow the news and politics. He became acquainted with the current topics of debate in the world, and with nothing to hold him back, he was swept into the rushing torrent of social controversy. The arguments of the reformers, with their vision of a world made perfect through the breaking of all restrictions, struck deep into his heart. His perception of himself and his place in the world underwent a sudden change, and soon he thought and dreamt of nothing but what brave new horizons they might bring.

As they becamed more involved with the town community, the three boys acquired new friends whose Jewish identity was "cultural" rather than religious, and they spent time conversing with these new friends on all manner of topics. They would evaluate every event in the outside world for its potential effect on the developments they considered to be the theme of the times. In the course of these discussions, Menachem came to hear the names of the leading authors of Greek and European thought. His command of Hungarian rapidly improved, he gained a knowledge of French and German with an ease that surprised him, and soon he was in possession of the basic trends of history, philosophy and literature. It seemed to him that the hours he passed in this way were the most exciting and meaningful he had ever spent, and though his Torah learning did not depart from his mind, he had placed it in a compartment of its own. He felt it was better like that. Why had he devoted himself to it as if it were the sole true value, he wondered, when there were other values without the same burden of work and responsibility?

And meanwhile, Elya was still oblivious of all this, still making his home in the spiritual worlds, following in the path of Moshe Chaim Sonnenschein, whose true level he was only beginning to appreciate. From time to time, he wondered what he would eventually do with his life, but all along he was secretly hoping that his *yeshivah* years would last forever.

It was, however, not long before an intimation of future demands came to him. One morning, they were sitting together at their studies, when his *chavrusa* was handed an official letter from Vienna. Moshe Chaim turned pale on seeing it, and when he opened it his worst fears were realized; it was a conscription letter, ordering him to report for drafting into the army. Elya took it from his hand and read:

> 10 March, 1866
> You have been called by order of His Imperial Majesty to present yourself for examination to determine your fitness for military service. The examination will be held at the Central Barracks, Pressburg, at the time stated below.

Moshe Chaim could think of only one man who might help him evade the military demand. Reb Chaim Halberstam, the Rebbe of Sanz and author of the *Divrei Chaim*, had once visited a nearby spa to bathe in the healing waters, and the Ksav Sofer, being unable to leave the *yeshivah* in person, had asked a select group of students to go there to pay the Rebbe his respects. Both Elya and Moshe Chaim had been among that group, and neither could forget the impression the meeting had made on them. The mere mention of the name of the Rebbe was enough to send shivers of awe down Moshe Chaim's spine.

Bidding his *Rosh Yeshivah* and friends a solemn farewell Moshe Chaim left for Sanz. He was confident that a blessing from the Rebbe would save him from his predicament. On arriving in Sanz, he went straight to the Rebbe's home, and as he entered the house and began to put down his bundle, he suddenly heard the voice of the *tzaddik* calling out from within.

"Young man, is it you whom they wish to appoint as general in the Emperor's army, when you have already been appointed as general of the Holy Land?"

Moshe Chaim stood rooted to the spot, scarcely daring to breathe as the voice continued.

"When you get home, do not forget to put a bandage on your foot."

The young leader, Moshe Chaim, listened carefully without moving as the *tzaddik* gave him his blessing, and he went on his way back to Pressburg.

Back in *yeshivah,* the day arrived for the fateful appointment, and before walking to the high-walled barracks in the center of the town, Moshe Chaim reminded himself of the instructions he had been given by the *tzaddik.* As he went he felt a tingling sensation making its way from his back down to the sole of his foot. His leg began to itch, and then before his eyes it swelled until it was grossly enlarged. By the time he reached the barracks, he could barely stagger in past the sentries.

The doctor who examined him gasped with horror when he saw his foot, and in less than five minutes, he was out in the street again carrying his exemption certificate, with a warning to lie down if he valued his life. On reaching home he took a bandage and wrapped it around his foot as he had been told. Almost as soon as it was in place, the pain and itching began to subside, and within half an hour the swelling was gone. His normal health had been completely restored.

In deep gratitude to *Hashem* and His holy servant the Rebbe of Sanz, Moshe Chaim Sonnenschein decided that the time had come for him to get married. He announced publicly that he would accept the first *shidduch* that would be offered to him, whereupon one of the *bachurim* present immediately suggested his own sister Sarah. True to his undertaking, Moshe Chaim accepted the proposal, and soon after the wedding, he left Pressburg with his bride. He immediately set out on the path that was to take him to the leadership of Yerushalayim itself.

This amazing sequence of events took Elya by the shoulders and spun him round until he was dizzy. In the blinking of an eye he had lost his cherished *chavrusa* to a miraculous providence, to a level far higher than his own. While he did not begrudge the sacrifice, he had been left alone in the *yeshiva,* and suddenly Pressburg itself had lost its savor for him. He realized that he too had to set out on the road of life, and after thinking the matter over he reckoned that he could do no better than to follow the example of his friend. He sought the approval of Reb Shimon Blau, and then he cabled his parents that he would soon be returning home. He asked them to begin looking for a suitable partner in marriage.

# CHAPTER SIX

*P*urim in Pressburg was a time of unrestrained celebration, a contrast to the disciplined and purposeful spirit which usually reigned in the *yeshivah*. The winter, too, was blowing itself out through its last wild gusty days. Storm after storm swept down on the city, but soon a hint of warmth could be detected even in the gales themselves, and it was clear that their force and fury had gone. The days of relief were at hand, with the first hesitant buds appearing on the trees and tiny white flowers piercing through the snow as it lay melting on the ground.

Elya was in a happy mood on one such morning as he made his way to the *Bais Medrash*, and when he saw his brother coming out of a side street with a somewhat downcast expression, he went over to him and took his arm to walk together with him, hoping to tell him the news of his plans. Smiling, he looked towards the sun that shone faintly upon them through the morning haze.

"Remember what Rashi says?" he said. "That Hashem brought the Jews out of Egypt in *Nissan* because it was the best time to go out of doors!"

Menachem nodded but did not reply. Elya peered at him more closely and saw that his words had not found favor. Gently he asked his brother why, and Menachem stopped walking and thought for a moment before he answered.

"You talk of going out of Egypt when there is oppression all around us," he said seriously. "All the peoples of the world are enslaved, and what is Rashi going to do to help them?"

Elya shrank back, startled. He was completely confused for a moment. A sense of hopelessness mingled with anger rose up in him, but he fought it down, struggling for words that would convey understanding and kindness to the brother whom he now saw slipping away before his eyes. He took Menachem's hand in his own.

"My brother," he said. "Rashi is telling us to look at the spring. Look around you. Don't you see the spring and the happiness it brings?"

Menachem turned to face his brother, and with a shock Elya realized he was not what he had been. His eyes were tired and careworn, yet there was a light within them of a kind Elya did not quite understand. It seemed to be a light of hope, but hope of a strange kind, agitated and without serenity.

"Yes, Elya, I see the spring," Menachem said. "And I, too, know what it means. It means the breaking of the shackles of winter from the hands of humanity. I know the part I have to play in this, and I know where I must go and what I must do."

"You're . . . you're leaving?" Elya stammered.

"I am going to Budapest. I have secured a place there to train as a lawyer. My friends here also have friends, and they know people in Budapest who are ready to receive me."

It seemed later to both of them that they stood there looking at each other for a long time, but in fact it could not have been more than half a minute, Elya examining every detail of his brother's face while Menachem stood with his jaw set firm and a look of patience in his eyes. Elya pulled himself together and shook his head.

"This won't do! What about our parents? What do you think they are going to have to say about this?"

"I haven't told them yet," replied Menachem. "I thought I would tell you first when there was an opportunity, and you would see to it that they didn't get too much of a shock."

"How am I supposed to do that?" cried Elya. "Do you think they will be able to let you go without speaking to you themselves?"

"All right," Menachem agreed. "Send them a telegram, and they can come here themselves. I won't leave until we've all talked it over. But you have to understand that it's not possible for me to discuss it at home."

Elya sighed wearily. "I suppose so, then."

He rubbed his chin, fingering the wisps of beard that had lately begun to appear there.

What should I do? he thought. Threaten him? No good at all. Show sadness? He'd pity me. What can I quote to him? It's no use. He's just gone deaf.

His heart stirred within him in pity for his brother, and his lips murmured a prayer. He gave Menachem a wan smile and raised his hand in farewell as he headed towards the post office in the center of the town to send off the telegram.

# CHAPTER SEVEN

When Chaim and Feige received Elya's cable it took them quite a few hours to compose themselves for the journey and for what lay ahead. Their emotions did not quite overpower them, but they knew there was little hope that they would meet with success in Pressburg. The event itself seemed to them to fit in with the whole difficult aspect of the world in which they were living, simply another disaster people had come to expect.

Chaim's thoughts went back to Budapest all those years ago, to the little boy whose hand he had taken from the hand of Kossuth. Menachem had looked up at him with a long stare, half expectant and half doubtful, as if already set on some path whose end he did not know. What were the dangers and pitfalls of this world beside the truths of eternity? The parents sat half-silent and disconsolate in the post wagon that took them to Budapest and in the boat along the Danube, knowing that they had a role to play in which they must not falter. After all, who knew whether they might not be able to hold their son back from his youthful rashness until some other influence could be brought to bear?

They arrived in Pressburg on the eve of *Shabbos Hagadol*, with five days left till *Pesach*. Elya had already told them that he would try to make arrangements for the *Sedarim*. By the time they arrived, he had found them two rooms in a house whose owners were leaving for *Yom Tov*, and so they would be able to make the *Seder* for themselves. They began to cherish a faint hope that in these surroundings they might be able to make Menachem change his mind.

Shortly thereafter, when they all met together for the first time in Elya's lodgings it was easy to see that Menachem still loved his parents. He and his father kissed each other tenderly and his concern for his mother was genuine. *Minchah* had just finished, and they sat talking in the gathering dusk about their memories of Grossverdan, the conversation becoming more and more intimate as the oil lamps began to wink out from behind the windows. Together, they ate a meal of potatoes and cream cheese, and as they sat over glasses of tea, Chaim decided it was time to tackle the subject uppermost in his mind. Beckoning Menachem over, he spoke to him quietly, so that the others could not hear what they were saying.

"Please don't start to think that we are unaware of what is happening in the world," he began. "I have lived in Budapest myself, and I know what the temptations are, but you must not get the idea that the simple devoted life of Torah and *mitzvos* is just a thing of the past."

Menachem flushed at this and put his glass down on the table.

"All I know is where my own capabilities lie," he murmured, staring down at the empty plate next to his hand.

"All respect to your capabilities," replied his father, "but that is not all that I know. You have spent some time here at a great *yeshivah*. Do you really think that the men here have no comprehension of what this means?"

"If they have, I have seen no sign of it," said Menachem with a touch of impatience.

"Not everything is so obvious at first sight. Your horizons will soon become very narrow if you restrict yourself to these first impressions. Is that the way of a man of intellect?"

Chaim smiled, and raised an eyebrow slightly.

Menachem also smiled shyly. "Apparently not."

"Very well, then. All that glitters is not gold."

Chaim hesitated for a moment at the decisive step and then spoke again.

"Why don't you come back to stay with us for a while and think things over?" he said. "If you go into the city now you will have no money, no standing of your own there. Come back to Grossverdan and relax a little, and make a bit of your own living in the business. You are very tense now, and that is not a state for making decisions."

Menachem stirred uneasily in his chair. He had to hand it to his father. The comments on the difficulties of his proposal had been precisely the ones whose implications he had been hoping to avoid, and there was no mistaking the concern that had prompted them. But would he be compromising his lifetime independence if he accepted? Would he ever be able to make a career to call his own if he did not move right away?

He tried to consider the proposal rationally, but suddenly he realized in the presence of his family how lonely he had really been through all these cold months, in a strange town with so many bewildering demands. He would be risking his happiness if he left the circle of the family so suddenly, and he would damage it so much that neither he nor they would have anything left to return to. Surely, he would lose nothing if he went back to pause for breath, and his father was not the kind of man who would exert unwelcome pressure. But somehow, he was still afraid, worried that the scenes of his childhood would drag him back into the state of mind from which he was longing to emerge.

He raised his eyes, smiling faintly.

"I can't go back to Grossverdan," he said. "I'm sorry, but I just can't."

He shrugged and turned away, and Chaim came to a decision at the gesture.

"Then we'll go somewhere else, all of us," he said. "We shall find some other place and make a new start together. Elya has decided to stay with us while he looks for a wife, and he can do that in plenty of places besides in Grossverdan." He regarded his son sternly but with a hint of a smile. "What do you say, then?"

Menachem nodded slowly and then made up his mind.

"All right, I'll give it a try."

Chaim breathed a sigh of relief, and they both leaned forward and shook hands. Leaving Menachem to sit for a while, Chaim got up and went over to where his wife was sitting with Elya. She rose quickly on seeing him, and they went over to the bay window for discussion.

Feige's eyes opened wide when she heard of the offer to move the whole family, and she started to say something, but then she took a cooler look at her husband and saw properly what was at stake. Chaim explained what had passed in his conversation.

"It was like a miracle," he said. "I didn't know what I was going to say, but the words just came straight to me."

"But what's going to happen?" Feige asked him. "Are we going to have to watch him every minute of the day in case he decides to leave?"

Chaim raised a hand despairingly to heaven. "Who knows? All I can say is that some kind of providence is working in our favor."

Hopeful and wondering, they parted for the night, with few words but much confidence from their family reunion.

Their *Seder* was a serious affair, but underlying it was a joyful expectation that carried them along. Menachem told his father afterwards that it had been an unforgettable experience.

# CHAPTER EIGHT

During the fine summer of that year, the Eisenstadt family made their move to the town of Huszt in the north of Hungary. This was a larger town than Grossverdan, a noted local center with quite an important Oberland Jewish community, and Chaim decided to go into business there.

They were all relieved to find themselves in fresh surroundings. It was a time when the whole world was breathing freely again around them. The American Civil War had just ended, and that meant the ceasing of many strains which had been troubling society. Adequate supplies of cotton became available with the end of the blockade on the South, and so the textile mills of Europe began working once more. America's own wealth was freed from war duty, spreading prosperity throughout the world, and the whole of the West became open for settlement. Immigrants came pouring across the ocean, most of them from Central Europe, and many of those who came were hard-working and enterprising people who had been held down in their careers by reactionary governments and restrictive conditions. The authorities in Europe were relieved to see so many potential reformers packing their bags, but by now they had given up any real attempt to stem the flow of progress.

The liberal Victorian era had begun. Educated and prosperous, its values were an advertisement for the virtues of the rising middle classes whose enterprise lay at the heart of the changes. The ideas of reform now occupied the mind of the Establishment, not just a gathering of radicals. Hostility and conflict were consigned to the past, and the stage seemed set for a secular triumph, not militant but more neglectful of spiritual things than it was prepared to acknowledge.

As Chaim set about building his new home, he, like so many others, felt a confidence in the expanding world around him, but at the heart of this feeling was an anxiety, a misgiving that he felt most keenly when he looked at Menachem. What kind of era could it be if it posed such a deadly threat to the integrity of his loved ones? He tried to reinforce his learning and his knowledge against the prevalent opinions, but he knew that all he could really do was to go forward in simple faith, come what may.

There were so many Jews in Huszt that the whole economy of the region could not have functioned without them. Some were small or medium scale moneylenders, some served as stewards and business agents on the estates of the nobility, but the majority were merchants and tradesmen, selling everything the peasant bought and buying everything that he sold. Such were the Jews of northern Hungary, men who went about in fear of their surroundings and yet dwelt in security, tavern keepers deeply immersed in the *Gemara*, bailiffs into whose hands had fallen sole charge over the lives of the degenerate noblemen whose lands they supervised.

As a newcomer, Chaim had no settled place in this intricate hierarchy, but in the new conditions he found himself a business opportunity, selling timber shingles for roofing. The business soon grew to a moderate volume, and by the time *Rosh Hashanah* came he was feeling quite secure. He made Menachem a partner, and the young man seemed to find some satisfaction in the steady activity as a contrast to his frenetic thinking in the *yeshivah*. He kept daily *mitzvah* observances without any appearance of strain.

A glorious November came to the countryside, beautiful sunny days with a nip in the air, more charming even than the spring because it was unexpected, and because one knew it would not last for long. The family had made friends with their nearest neighbors. One of these families was the Schustermans, a retired couple from Pressburg who had come to live near their nephew, a local man named Teitelbaum with whom Chaim regularly learned *Gemara*. The other neighbors were the Friedmans, a large bustling family, headed by a man of Chaim's own age with a flourishing business in the sale of paprika to Budapest. His wife Ettie would cheerfully take under her wing anyone within her field of vision who seemed to have need of a little care and attention. Thus she did with Feige, and the women were always in each other's houses, exchanging life histories and insights on life's twists and turns.

Needless to say, the ages and situations of their children were among the earliest topics of discussion, and as Feige thought of Elya, she began to regard the Friedmans' eldest daughter Bayla with something more than passing interest. Bayla was indeed a sight on which any mother's eye might rest with a good deal of tenderness. Slightly above medium height, with plain braids and full brown eyes in a pale complexion, she combined her mother's cheerfulness with an idealism and composure that placed her firmly in a class of her own. She had spoken a little with Feige in her mother's presence, and Feige had been considerably impressed by her strength of character. Feige herself was fully familiar with Torah, and when the conversation touched on such topics she was pleased to find herself in the company of an intellectual equal. A feeling began to grow within her that the divine purpose in making marriages might have been well served by their arrival in this town.

On one of these November mornings, Bayla and her mother were working together making jam and preserves for the winter, from the raspberries and plums the local market gardeners had brought to sell in the town. Bayla was piercing the whole fruits with a needle before her mother rolled them in crushed sugar. On the stove, a big copper cauldron was boiling with sugar water and a handful of lemon pits tied in a muslin bag. Mother and daughter chatted quietly while they worked, enjoying their lifelong intimacy and the feeling of preparation for the long, hard and cold winter ahead. The baby played happily on the kitchen floor with a colorful noisy rattle.

"Mommie," said Bayla. "Why does a baby need toys that make noise?"

Ettie laughed. "You might just as well ask why anyone ever makes a noise. A baby feels insecure with only its own voice to rely on."

"If I had my own baby I'd never let it feel I was out of reach," said Bayla.

Ettie took a sidelong glance at her daughter for a moment. Yes, there she was, seventeen years old and starting to talk about the future. She wasn't the kind of girl who would have any difficulty finding a *shidduch*. Could this be the moment to bring up the subject?

"Bayla," she began as the girl turned her head. "What kind of a man would you like to spend your life with?"

Bayla rested her hands on the table and tossed away a wisp of hair from her brow as she turned to face her mother.

"Oh, a *Ben Torah*, definitely. Someone whose knowledge is increasing all the time."

"And how will you manage to live, my dear?" inquired her mother.

"There'll be something. Some business, or even a rabbinic appointment. Rabbis are being paid much more these days, you know!" She smiled back triumphantly at her own practical knowledge.

"Well, then, if that's what you want we must find you a rabbi," said her mother briskly. A thought that had been at the back of her mind for some time suddenly crystallized. She wasn't sure if it was the right time to mention it. On second thought she spoke aloud.

"You know, Elya Eisenstadt next door left Pressburg with a very good name. Should I ask his mother what his plans might be for the future?"

Bayla stared back, her eyes wide. She had been in the room when Feige had described her son, and the same possibility had

## ON·TWO·FRONTS

occurred to her, too.

"Do you think he might be interested?" she asked slowly and carefully. She wouldn't have voiced her thoughts then, but now that her mother brought it up she allowed herself to express interest.

Ettie took her hand. "We must find out, must we not?"

# CHAPTER NINE

That very evening, Ettie went over to the Eisenstadts and proposed that their children should meet with a view to marriage. Elya was not surprised that an offer had been made, since it was with that particular purpose that he had come to Huszt. He was ready to accept Bayla simply on the strength of what he had heard of her qualities, and he looked forward to smoothing away any hesitations she might have about him. He was happy. Everything in his life seemed to be building up to this predestined conclusion, an end that was also a beginning. Already he considered himself as engaged, and he prayed for help in all the difficulties that might lie before him.

Bayla, on the other hand, was quite hesitant at the prospect of meeting a man with whom she might well be sharing her entire existence, and she withdrew into herself considerably in the days that followed. She wondered if this was really her predestined partner, and as she walked among the yellowing trees, lost in thought, she could only derive reassurance from those small aspects of her surroundings which she had known since her earliest childhood.

She felt she could not discuss these feelings in detail with her mother, and so she was greatly relieved when a distant cousin of hers, a regular visitor to the family, came to stay for a week or two. Zissie Levinsohn was a few months older than Bayla, and the two rejoiced in each other's company, partly because their very different temperaments complemented each other so well.

Orphaned as a child, Zissie had been brought up by an aunt and uncle who had gone to settle in Prague. Her early life had been full of the sights and sounds of the great city and the beauty of its setting on the river. She had formed an idea of life directed towards realizing the innate potential in her surroundings, and she was always ready to lend an ear to other people's troubles. She was vigorous and industrious, to an extent that even startled some people who saw her. At the same time she was devoted to Torah, and everyone hoped that in the right surroundings she would settle down very nicely, extending her influence far and wide to the benefit of all.

When Zissie heard the news of Bayla's forthcoming meeting she clasped her hands, beamed in delight and kissed her cousin on both cheeks.

"So there you are!" she exclaimed. "Everything is arranged!"

But her face grew serious when she looked more closely and saw that Bayla was even paler than usual and had obviously been losing sleep. She took Bayla's hand.

"Come on, let's go and sit down where no one can hear us," she said.

They drew their chairs into a corner of the room, and Zissie listened as Bayla began, at first hesitantly but soon more confidently, to convey her unsettled mood. As she finished, Zissie gave her a smile and put an arm around her shoulders.

"My darling, you have a strength in your soul that can help you overcome many things," she told her. "It cannot be that a man with so many wonderful qualities could fail in some little particular."

Bayla's face relaxed into a smile, and she glanced curiously at her cousin.

"You seem to know a lot about these things," she remarked. "How did you find out so much if you are still single?"

Zissie pursed her lips. "Oh, I don't know. My aunt and uncle are very kind to me, but I've still had to find my own way in most things."

Bayla laughed. "Don't worry, it's easy to see that you know what you are talking about. How do you see your future?"

Zissie stared towards the fire and made a dismissive gesture.

"I don't know," she said. "I just don't know. Maybe I'm not so easy to place. Most of the men from regular families never seem to have formed the kind of approach that I have had to."

"How unusual do you want to be?" asked Bayla.

Zissie shook her head. "Don't think I'm just trying to be special. I'm sure there's a man for me like there is for everybody, but where he's hiding himself I don't know."

Bayla's eyes grew large, and her voice took on a hushed and serious tone. She leaned closer to her friend.

"Shall I tell you something?" she said. "Elya has a brother who was in the *yeshivah* in Pressburg with him. His name is Menachem, and while he was there he was editing a newsletter on general topics, interesting things, with a couple of other friends. His parents were afraid that he was under bad influences, so they got him to come back here in case he did anything silly. But everyone says he has a good head, and he's idealistic, too. Couldn't he just be the one you're looking for?" She giggled. "And then we'd be sisters-in-law!"

Zissie sat for a long time lost in thought.

"So I'd be the one to see to it that he stayed on the right track?" she said at last.

"Yes, it does seem that way. It might suit you very well, too."

"All right, then. Tell your mother to ask his parents what they think, and I'll be ready to meet him if they agree."

Bayla threw her arms around her.

"It'll be perfect, you'll see! Nothing ever happens by accident, does it?"

When Chaim and Feige heard of this new development they were so amazed that they hardly dared hope that it would actually come to pass. Menachem smiled and raised no objections, and it was arranged that he and Zissie should meet in two weeks time, while his brother's meeting took place immediately.

## ON·TWO·FRONTS

And so Elya and Bayla found themselves on the following afternoon facing each other in front of the fire in the Friedmans' living-room, wearing their best clothes and sitting on the best chairs, with a table before them bearing glasses of tea, a pot of Bayla's newly prepared raspberry jam and a plate of crackers. The formalities of preparing and serving the tea helped to relax the nervousness which both of them were feeling acutely. However, it was not until they could feel the actual warmth of their first shared refreshment that they were able to talk to each other properly.

Elya began by asking Bayla to talk about her life, about the things she had thought and done as a child, and he soon saw the calm, pleasant way in which she saw people and relationships. By the time ten minutes had passed, he was sure he had within himself what would answer to her needs. He asked more questions, drawing her on and encouraging her thoughts, in personal concerns and in Torah, until she too saw that he had the key to her mind. She realized that she was in the presence of a man who by his very nature was no stranger to her. They talked on for an hour or so, smiling as they exchanged reminiscences. By the time it was over Bayla knew that this very conversation had brought her a whole stage further in her development. They parted with good wishes for the coming *Shabbos* and went to tell their parents of the hope that had emerged between them.

As the Friedmans observed their daughter that *Shabbos*, they could see that she was on the point of emerging from her cocoon of innocence. At the Eisenstadts, too, there was gladness at the thought that Elya might have found the partner with whom to embark on the wider prospects that beckoned to a young man of his abilities. When the week began, events between the two young people gathered pace very rapidly. They met once more, this time in the Eisenstadt home, and there were no barriers in the way of a complete agreement between them. After half an hour, they emerged full of smiles, with the news of an engagement.

Chaim and Elya embraced and kissed, shaking each other's hands in a firm, unbreakable grip, and then Elya kissed his mother, while Menachem stood beside them watching with a little smile on his face at the outpouring of emotion. Bayla ran next door to tell her mother, and soon the street echoed with screams of delight as the whole family danced and kissed and began to discuss plans as fast as they could talk.

There would be no problem with accommodations. Bayla's father owned a small house a few streets away, and the couple would be well placed there at least for the winter.

It was all so easy and straightforward. The *tena'im* were arranged for two weeks from that date, and a large number of relatives and friends from around the district were expected to gather in Huszt for the celebration. Everyone also agreed that the atmosphere of a large *simchah* would be the best way for Zissie and Menachem to make each other's acquaintance. Thus they prepared for the great occasion.

# CHAPTER TEN

On the night of the *tena'im*, the four Eisenstadts came into the bride's house together. They found it thronged with people, everyone with plenty of news to catch up on, and it seemed likely that at least two hours would pass over light food and drink before the time came for the formalities. Chaim beckoned to Bayla's father, and he brought Zissie's aunt and uncle over to them, together with their young charge. Zissie maintained her calm over nervous anticipation and managed to smile benevolently as Menachem came forward to meet her.

Elya and the others went their separate ways, and the two sat down facing each other in comfortable chairs in a corner of the next room. Neither of them had any idea of how to begin, and an uncomfortable silence fell as they regarded each other uneasily. Zissie fanned herself energetically with a handkerchief.

"It's hot in here," she remarked.

Menachem smiled as he saw an opportunity.

"If you'd been in the Pressburg Yeshivah during the winter you wouldn't mind how hot it was in here," he said.

She looked at him closely.

"What do you mean?" she asked.

He began to tell her all about the intense cold in the lodgings in Pressburg and the tricks the *bachurim* had thought up to avoid it. He talked on and on, describing the surroundings and the life of the Jewish town, and the hopes and ambitions that he himself had formed there. He was aware of an enormous feeling of relief at being able to talk freely about these things to someone his own age. And as he went on, he saw that she understood everything he was saying, that she shared his own level of awareness.

She listened with interest, asking a question here and there, and before long his reserve had disappeared completely. She could certainly see something impressive about him. Whether it was due to the teaching in the *yeshivah* or not, he undoubtedly had the knack of getting to the root of a problem. And he knew how to laugh, too. Her eyes sparkled as she saw the thread of irony and realism in his discourse. He knew people, places and things, and he spoke of them in a way that rang true.

Is it just an incidental meeting, Menachem thought as their doubts melted away, or are we really life partners? I've never felt so at ease with anyone. She's brought me out of my shell.

The clock against the wall struck nine, and they realized they had been talking for nearly an hour. Menachem had had to raise his voice to compete with the noise of the party, and now he was tired, the sweat pouring from his brow. He reached for his handkerchief, and he saw that she was grinning at him mischievously.

"Maybe it's too hot in here after all?" she said.

They laughed together, both happy at the wonderful new feeling of release from their tensions, knowing that they could always look to each other for more of the same. They stood up, took their leave and went off to tell their elders of the likely prospect of another marriage in the family.

Once the *tena'im* were over, the two families regarded themselves as related, and their relationship became very purposeful and practical. Zissie, however, tended to feel a little left out of this, and her feeling of rootlessness was increased by all the bustle and preparation around her. She knew that Menachem also was basically alone in the world, but until some actual arrangement was made with him she had no way of entering that aspect of his life and joining it with her own. Anxious and frustrated, she helped Bayla and her mother with the *trousseau*, waiting impatiently for her next meeting with the young man who held the hope of so much happiness.

By the time the second meeting between Zissie and Menachem was arranged, this time in the Eisenstadt home, the wind began to blow hard and cold. The days were short, fur coats appeared on the people's shoulders, and the trees were bleak and bare. Already there was a breath of snow in the air.

As Zissie sat looking out of the Eisenstadts' window waiting for Menachem to return from *Maariv*, neither the weather nor the delay were improving her mood. At last, he came in with his father, blowing on his hands and rubbing them together. He apologized for being late, went to prepare tea and busied himself with pouring it while his father went out and left the two of them alone.

They chatted for a while about the things that had happened since their last meeting, but the talk didn't seem to be leading anywhere. This time Zissie decided to take a firm hand.

"You did many different things in the *yeshivah*," she asked him suddenly, "but which of them do you really want to do?"

Menachem glanced up at her, frowning at having been placed on the spot, but then he saw the tension in her face.

"I think that journalism and publicity is what I do best," he answered quietly.

Zissie paused for a few moments, and then took the plunge.

"Your father lost you in 1848, during the invasion," she said. "Isn't that right?"

Menachem crossed his hands on his knee.

"Yes, that is so."

"And you were cared for by Kossuth and his wife?"

"Yes."

Zissie smiled, leaning forward as she spoke. "And so you want to be a journalist?"

Menachem laughed shortly.

"Not even Kossuth could make me into something I wasn't already."

Zissie leaned back again. "Well said! But do you still think of him as admirable? Are you in contact with him?"

"I have not seen or heard from him through all these years," replied Menachem steadily. "He probably does not even know where I am. Do I admire him? He is not an extremist any more. His ideals are shared by everyone."

Zissie caught his eye and chuckled.

"We are the younger generation," she said. "We still have our own ideals before us, do we not?"

"And you want to know about mine?"

She did not reply but gazed at him with intensity and frankness. He hesitated before answering.

"I believe in the Torah, but I suppose you might call me a universalist. I believe in Jewish observance but only insofar as people can benefit from it. There is a spirit in the heart of man which strives to break the bonds of confinement, and I am a friend of that spirit."

Zissie's eyes narrowed.

"Are you referring to Jews themselves?" she asked sharply.

"I believe that all of humanity is linked in a common bond," said Menachem, trying to calm her, "and that no one should reject what another may have to teach him. Who is wise? He who learns from everyone."

"What? Are you saying that the *goyim* have some teachings that Jews need?" Zissie started, almost rising out of her chair.

"It is known that they have wise men," replied Menachem carefully. "And I have not yet fully examined all that they might have to say."

Zissie leaped to her feet.

"Well don't expect me to sit around until you've found out what they have to say! Wise men of the *goyim*, indeed! Who told you such things?"

Menachem also rose to his feet and held up a hand to reassure her.

"Please, please, don't get angry," he pleaded. "I may not know all the answers yet, but I still have a bit of ability."

Zissie calmed down a little. She remained standing and eyed him cautiously.

"What would you want to do?" she asked.

"If we got married?"

"Yes."

"I was planning to go to Budapest and become a lawyer. Everybody has to earn a living, and there is no harm in taking part in activities for the betterment of the individual and the state. Nothing would make me happier than to do that with you as my wife."

All of Zissie's frustration welled up in her as she heard these words. All the fears she had nurtured through her youth were now brought to a head by this sudden offer that had proved so bitterly disappointing.

"Well, you can keep it!" she flared angrily. "I want a kosher home! I want a father who teaches his children the truth that our ancestors knew! Wise men of the *goyim*? You'll eat their meat! You'll drink their wine!"

She picked up her coat and made for the door. He followed her, protesting, and she paused with her hand on the knob, her expression softening for a moment.

"If you get wise you can come back and find me, but don't take too long, that's all."

In a flood of tears, she swept out of the house and ran next door to collapse on the sofa as Bayla and her mother ran to help her in consternation.

The sudden reversal in the tide of events greatly upset the families. Elya and Bayla's marriage plans still had to go forward, and this only increased the feelings of guilt that Zissie and Menachem were now bearing. Zissie knew that she had flown off the handle, and Menachem was also aware that more lay behind her outburst than his own plans. But now that they had clashed openly they were pushed back onto their own resources, and each had despaired of getting any help from the other.

The Friedmans persuaded Zissie to stay on in Huszt in the hope of a reconciliation, but she moped all day and would hardly eat. Menachem was reluctant to leave her, but he was finding it difficult to stay on in the town in the face of the very real objections she had made to the direction his life was taking. Eventually, he decided to go to Budapest as he had planned. He told his parents about his decision, and when they saw that he was set on it, they agreed to let him go on condition that he remained in constant touch by letter.

Elya and Bayla served as messengers between Zissie and Menachem in the last few days before his departure. Zissie asked to tell him that she still hoped for his return and that she would not make other plans for the meantime until she was sure which way his decision had gone. When Menachem heard this he was deeply touched that the girl who was now the most important person in his life had stayed loyal to him under very difficult circumstances. Still he had no clear way in which to justify her affections. It was a dilemma. He sent a message to her saying that he hoped to succeed in all that was required of him in life, and he asked her to bear with him for a while until he knew properly what that might be.

# CHAPTER ELEVEN

*I*n the winter of 1866, the turns of fortune were bringing happy times to Budapest. Hungary's rich deposits of coal and iron were being exploited by the new railways, and thus the whole country was turning to an industrial way of life. Capitalism had come to sweep away the old aristocratic domination and the oppression of the peasants, and there was no doubt that people were getting richer as a consequence. Fine new avenues were being constructed in the city, with grand public buildings and statues, and all the bustling life of a Western capital. World famous professors lectured in the universities on the exciting new developments in science, to students who were ready to use their knowledge effectively. Everywhere the romantic music of the great composers was being played and sung.

However, not everyone was happy. Dark slums festered in the

industrial areas, riddled with degradation and crime, where Anarchist gangs plotted their bombings and assassinations, where the resentful legions of organized labor prepared for Communist takeover, where gutter agitators began to spout the lunatic ideas that Fascism and Nazism would later bring to power.

To Menachem, however, it seemed once more, as he trod through the piles of snow in the streets under a friendly winter sunshine, that spring was just around the corner. He was young, and the world that lay before him was a world of opportunity. Lately, he had become more aware of his own appearance, and as he found the street name he was looking for and strode off confidently through the crowds, he was sure that anyone who met him would judge him favorably by the appearance he presented.

There was a coffee house down a side street where he knew his friends were usually to be found, and when he came through the door, he was not disappointed. Scanning the faces around the marble-topped tables, he immediately recognized the man he was looking for, and just at the same moment, the other looked up and spotted him, too.

"Menachem! *Vos machst du?*" he cried, raising his hand in greeting. "So you got here, heh? Come and sit down. Waiter! Two glasses of coffee!"

When the waiter set the steaming brew in front of him, Menachem hesitated only a moment before raising it silently to his lips. After all, what difference could it make? He was here, and he needed a hot drink. It was a cold day.

"What's that you're buried in?" he asked his friend, pointing to the book on the table.

"This? It's a history of the papacy. A French Protestant wrote it. You should read it. Very interesting."

"Plenty of funny business there, eh?"

"That's what they always told us," said the other, and they both laughed.

They sat together quietly for a while over the warm drinks, savoring the intimate atmosphere of the little coffee house. Menachem breathed the air deeply, relaxing for the first time in a long while. He spoke again to his friend.

"So, then, Laibie," he said. "What's doing these days?"

## ON·TWO·FRONTS

Laibie leaned back with a satisfied smile on his face.

"Well, you know, we manage somehow. We try to improve our minds a little. How about you?"

"I've come here to start off my life," Menachem replied. A gleam came into his eye. "I was in the *yeshivah* in Pressburg, but it wasn't fulfilling enough. I stayed with my parents for a while. I met a girl there, but she didn't care for where I was going in life."

"And where might that be?" asked Laibie quizzically.

"I was editing a magazine, and you know how these things can turn out. It gave me a look into publicity and causes, and I thought that if I qualified in law here I could become active in a lot of interesting things."

Laibie nodded. "There certainly isn't a shortage of causes. And it isn't so hard for Jewish people to get ahead as it used to be. You can find yourself among *chevrah* wherever you go. How do you feel about things, anyway?"

Menachem shrugged a shoulder and smiled.

"What can I say? It's nice to be Jewish. But there's something going on with Jewish life that isn't quite so simple. People seemed to fade out of the strict observances just at the exact time when the outside world decided to emancipate us. We were always told that Judaism was eternal, but all of a sudden it seems not to be."

Laibie also smiled. "What do we know? Maybe we are living an illusion. But if there is anyone who knows the answer, he isn't here to tell us."

"Life is an illusion," said Menachem philosophically. "It's just a question of the form you choose. The underlying values are all the same. One has to fulfill oneself and help others fulfill themselves."

Laibie beckoned to the waiter and ordered two more coffees.

"You know, there are plenty of people on the religious side who talk like you're talking now," he said. "It's called the Reform movement. They try to give people the kind of religion they want in today's conditions. If you took up that cause you'd find plenty to do. There's a whole new philosophy being worked out, with books and articles being written, for modern education and to publicize the new ideas. Even the government is interested. They're not short of money either, I can tell you."

Menachem chuckled deprecatingly. "Well now, that's always a

consideration, I suppose. Can you put me in touch with them?"

Laibie sat up and began to look important.

"Yes, I can, if you want me to," he said. "Most of the leaders are in Germany, but they are starting to set up representation here in Budapest. There are two or three men here who have a professorial status in their own right, and they'd be glad to talk to you, I'm sure."

They drank their coffee for a while and talked quietly about the whereabouts of friends and the current topics in town. When Menachem rose to leave, his friend took him to the door, and they shook hands.

"Get fixed up at the University, and I'll be in touch in a couple of weeks," said Laibie.

"I'll be waiting to hear from you," replied Menachem, and he grinned. "It looks as though the good times are just starting!"

"Let's hope so," Laibie answered, serious as always, and they said goodbye.

Menachem took lodgings near the University, in the house of an old German woman who smoked a pipe. He ate meager meals in coffee houses, anxious all the time over how long his savings would last. He had registered at the University and was attending his first courses in the law of the land. It was stodgy material, but he felt he was doing what was necessary in order to realize his ideals. He worked quite hard and formed a circle of friends, both Jews and non-Jews, who had all come from obscure origins in the provinces and were looking forward to life in the great city.

About two weeks later Laibie came to see him, and they went out for a stroll by the river. Laibie came straight to the point.

"You're in luck," he said. "I've arranged an interview for you with Moshe Gottfried. He's one of the leading publicists for the Reform movement, in touch with all the big men in Germany. I told him you had been in a *yeshivah* and edited a paper there. He didn't waste any time, and he told me to bring you on Thursday evening."

Menachem fairly boiled with excitement.

"Of course, I'll come!" he exclaimed. "Will you meet me here?"

"Yes, I will," replied Laibie, smiling at his friend's enthusiasm, and they went off to raise a glass of good beer to the future.

# CHAPTER TWELVE

Doctor Gottfried, as was his full title, lived on the other side of the river in the suburb of Pest. As Menachem crossed the bridge with Laibie a feeling of apprehension mingled with his hopes. He had never been in this new section of the city before, and it represented everything about the modern life that was so far from his origins.

They rang the bell at the door of a modest town house, and Gottfried himself came to answer the call. Smiling broadly, he took them into his study and sat them down, amid a clutter of books in several languages. Meanwhile he busied himself clearing up the papers on a desk whose most conspicuous feature was a large brass ink stand in the shape of a German eagle. Finally, he sat down and turned to Laibie, still smiling.

"So this is the young man?"

## ON·TWO·FRONTS

Laibie replied in the affirmative, and in the light of the desk lamp, Menachem had his first opportunity to study the features of the Doctor as he turned his face towards him. He was past middle age, short and thin, with a slightly sallow complexion, and his hair grew down over a bald pate into little curls at the back of his neck. He wore a belted silk dressing gown over his shirt and trousers. His moustache was shaven, but his chin bore a silvery goatee beard which at this time of the evening was somewhat less than tidy, and though his lips smiled constantly, his eyes did not always follow the smile but roved around the room, peering intently over his spectacles at people or furniture that caught his attention.

Now, he was peering at Menachem, and the perpetual smile widened to include him in its welcome.

"Well now, my young friend! You are a budding editor, I believe?"

Menachem nodded, unable to reply. The man was pleasant enough, but there was something about him that seemed somehow out of place. His speech was rapid and precise, in Oberland Yiddish with a noticeable German accent.

"A great profession," murmured Gottfried, still holding Menachem with his eyes. "Everything depends on the written word. So well do I remember Doctor Moses Mendelssohn of happy memory, who would always say how everything could be achieved with the proper choice of words."

Menachem was beginning to feel a little out of his depth, but he nodded again and glanced sideways at Laibie, who smiled reassuringly.

"I have always enjoyed writing," Menachem managed to say.

"Quite, quite," purred the publicist, calming him with a wave of the hand. "The main thing is that you should enjoy it, and I am happy to say that if you are willing we can give you many things to do that you will enjoy."

Menachem was now starting to find himself.

"What kind of things?" he asked tentatively.

"Ah, well," replied Gottfried, settling back in his deep chair. He assumed a judicious expression and looked at the ceiling for a moment, pressing the tips of his fingers together. "We are engaged in many campaigns of the greatest importance. We have to convince

## ON·TWO·FRONTS

both the Jewish and the non-Jewish public of the value of ethical conduct, over and above the mere outward trappings of observance. To this end, we place many articles in the columns of newspapers whose editors are sympathetic to us, and we are lobbying several governments to change the school system in a suitable way. Education itself is changing all over the world from the forms it has had since the Middle Ages, and we are at the center of these encouraging trends. The value of the exact sciences, the logical approach to human studies and so forth. At all events we must match the external emancipation by emancipating ourselves from the backward elements that remain in our midst." He turned to Menachem, who had been listening with attention. "Perhaps you might tell me where your interests most closely lie?"

"I am not really sure," Menachem answered, gesturing with his hand to break the tension he felt gathering in the room. "If you could suggest something . . ."

Gottfried thought for a moment.

"There is a well-respected paper in Buda which sometimes carries our articles," he said. "It is under the editorship of a close follower of Kossuth."

Menachem jumped.

"Kossuth?" he exclaimed, staring wildly.

"Yes, Kossuth," Gottfried replied, somewhat surprised. "You will have heard of him. Do you know him personally?"

"Er, I . . . I have not seen him for many years," stammered Menachem. "No, no, I do not know him."

"Very well, then," answered Gottfried, apparently satisfied. "He is not one of our supporters, but as a matter of democratic principle, he does not exclude our viewpoint from publicity. I would like you to write an article for this paper on . . . let me see . . . yes . . . the loyalty of Jews to their home countries in time of war and to take it to this editor for his approval. I will write you a note to bring along."

He took a piece of paper and bent to his desk, his forehead shining in the lamplight.

"There!" He handed the note to Menachem. "And G-d be with you, my boy. I trust that this is the start of a great and fruitful career."

He stood up and came around the desk to where Menachem and Laibie now stood, and he grasped Menachem by the hand.

## ON·TWO·FRONTS

"Everywhere our movement is expanding!" the Doctor continued. "All Germany now follows our creed! Across the ocean our Hebrew Union College is spreading the word in Cincinnati, and Doctor Kaufmann Kohler is doing great work from his pulpit in Temple Emanu-El in the city of New York. Be with us, young man! Be one of our number!"

He gave Menachem's hand a final wring, his spectacles shining with fervor, and the interview was over.

When Gottfried had closed the door on them after patting Laibie on the shoulder and thanking him for bringing along such a promising young helper, the two boys stood together out in the street in complete silence. Laibie seemed to be waiting for Menachem to voice his feelings, but Menachem was disinclined to do so. He just stood there tight-lipped. Eventually, Laibie found his voice and asked his friend how he thought things had gone.

"Are they all like that?" asked Menachem in reply.

"Not necessarily," said Laibie carefully. "It takes all sorts, you know."

"Possibly," said Menachem. "I suppose the big world just takes a bit of getting used to."

They walked slowly back to the bridge, each absorbed in his own thoughts, and parted with restrained courtesies on the other side of the shimmering moonlit river.

# CHAPTER THIRTEEN

Menachem took a good deal of care over his article. He rewrote it three times, but he did not show it to anyone else for approval. When he could no longer bear to change anything more, he copied it out neatly and took it, along with the note he had been given, to the newspaper office near the center of the city. He climbed one flight of stairs and found himself in a little dusty, unkempt office full of activity, with people coming and going all the time. The editor was sitting at a desk near the window and greeted Menachem cheerfully when he introduced himself.

"Wait here a minute," he told Menachem upon reading Gottfried's note. "I will take this to our cultural editor."

He left the room with a batch of papers, and Menachem sat down nearby, taking in the scene with growing interest as the minutes ticked by. He was feeling caught up in the atmosphere of journalism that had always attracted him, the breezy confidence and the sense of being up to the minute with the latest delights and surprises. However, there was one worrying thought at the back of his mind concerning this visit, and he was not surprised to hear it confirmed when one of the reporters said to another, "Ask Mister Laszos Kossuth when he gets here."

A few minutes later, he saw a grey haired man in a frock coat enter the room. All those present looked up and nodded their greetings. Menachem did likewise. Kossuth acknowledged his presence and then went up to one of the reporters to discuss the business on which he had come. Menachem watched the conversation with a growing sense of unease.

He sat in his chair, and Kossuth caught sight of him again as he finished. Seeing the wary look in Menachem's eye, he asked the reporter,

"Who is this?"

The reporter replied that Menachem had been sent to them with an article by Moshe Gottfried, and Kossuth smiled and came over with an outstretched hand.

"I hope we will see more of you here," he said. "What is your name?"

Menachem told him, and Kossuth stood rooted to the spot, staring in amazement. Slowly, he raised his hand and rubbed his chin, and then he lowered it again and spoke.

"I never thought I would see you again," he said quietly. "Are you well?"

"Yes, thank you," Menachem replied. "I am well."

"How is your father?"

"He is also well."

"Are you in touch with him?" asked Kossuth, his eyes narrowing as he regarded Menachem more closely, noticing the rumpled clothes and the clean-shaven face.

"He knows where I am," said Menachem equably.

Kossuth looked at him steadily.

"Your father is one of the finest men I have ever met," he said. "I wonder what his opinion would be concerning a son who dressed in this manner."

"I cannot speak for him," Menachem answered, jutting out his jaw. "I am my own master."

Kossuth looked at him a moment longer and then drew him over to a chair next to one of the tables. They sat down, and inspected each other as the men in the room went back to their tasks. Kossuth put his elbow on the table and leaned over towards Menachem.

"I know Moshe Gottfried," he said quietly. "He is a highly educated man. There are many like him whose acquaintance I have made in my time. I would say that most of them rate higher in the scale than he does."

Menachem squared his shoulders.

"You are being quite blunt about it," he said. "Why do you speak to me this way?"

"I speak this way, young man," said Kossuth, "because I have had many contacts with the Jewish people over the years, and I am not in doubt over what it is that makes them what they are."

Menachem turned his head on one side.

"Please tell me what it is?" he asked, bristling.

"Now, now, calm down," said Kossuth soothingly. "I don't mean to browbeat you. But I still have some thought for your welfare, and I can tell you that Moshe Gottfried and his associates do not know how to care for your welfare."

He looked intently at Menachem, who had again turned to face him and was listening apprehensively to his words.

"The good of the Jewish people is inseparable from their special observances, which keep them as a nation distinct from all others," Kossuth said firmly. "They do themselves a great disfavor by abandoning these distinctions at the behest of impulsive men whose knowledge is only shallow."

"But you are the great democrat!" Menachem burst out. "You have been the champion of equality all your life! And now you come to tell me that it is all nonsense and that the Brotherhood of Man is something in which the Jews can never share?"

Kossuth raised a hand to silence him.

"Now, please listen. The Jews should certainly not be placed under penal restrictions, but democracy still does not mean that everyone is the same. The Jews must now defend their beliefs in new circumstances, and democracy will allow them to do that. But to abandon everything they stand for as soon as they are out in the open is the sheerest folly. Plenty of people know this. Don't deceive yourself. And I am talking about Jews like you and your family, who are fortunate to be in full possession of their heritage."

Menachem sank back into the chair, his mind reeling. He cast agitated glances around the room, hoping for some inspiration, but none came, and suddenly under the stress a certainty presented itself to his mind.

"I can't do it!" he said to Kossuth, almost gasping. "It just doesn't feel right! Times are changing, and you have changed them as much as anyone. Don't you understand what it means, what is really at stake?"

Kossuth drew himself up.

"I have said what I thought you should hear. The times are surely turbulent, and it is hard to find a place to stand, let alone a direction. But the years since I last saw you have taught me more firmly what I knew even then, and I am glad I have been allowed to remedy any harm I may have done you by affirming it here and now. I would advise you not to discard your heritage."

So saying, he rose to his feet, leaving Menachem staring up at him from the chair. He took his leave of the office with a smile and a bow, and then he turned his back and was gone.

A few days later, Menachem received a letter from the cultural editor, saying that the article had been accepted. After the encounter with Kossuth though, Menachem did not feel the excitement he had thought he would. He kept on with his law studies, enjoying the social life of the university circle, but somehow a monotony had crept into it, and he began to feel a little depressed. He tried to tell himself that it was inevitable in the big city, alone against the world with only his own potential to live on, but he was experiencing more and more homesickness, and on more than one occasion, his thoughts turned to Zissie. While he had been in the thick of his commitments, he had convinced himself that he was doing the best thing for her also, but now that he remembered her words to him he was not so sure. He started wondering where she was and whether she still thought of him from time to time.

In fact, she was still in Huszt where he had left her, living under the roof of Bayla's parents, yet more a part of the young household of

## ON·TWO·FRONTS

Elya and Bayla themselves. She and Bayla were together almost every day, and she was learning from her cousin what married life really involved. As a result, Zissie lost some of her impulsiveness and became more reflective. Her heart was more open to Torah study, and she began to see in it a beauty, different from the worldly beauty that had animated her early days.

Elya was going "from strength to strength." He learned, understood and added to his knowledge, and soon he was a young *Rav* whose name was spoken of in the town. For all their worry over Menachem, from whom they continued to receive noncommittal notes scrawled on pieces of paper, Chaim and Feige were much gratified by the advancement of their other son. A deep contentment developed in their lives, continuing to grow as events and seasons came and went.

# CHAPTER FOURTEEN

*E*lya had formed a relationship with Reb Aryeh Feldman, the brother of the town *Rav*, Reb Yechezkel Feldman, a man with a philosophical mind and an enthusiast's determination to uphold truth at every different turn in the path. They had many discussions together, in Reb Aryeh's home or walking together in the woods around the town, on current issues and on the paths taken by great *tzaddikim* of the generation. Elya found himself putting his heart and soul into these discussions. He especially admired the settled quality of his teacher's mind, which always seemed to embody peace even from within the twists and the turmoil of conflict.

Reb Aryeh also saw the acuity with which the young man responded to the questions in hand, and he gave lengthy thought in considering what direction it might be best to send him. Should he be a town *Rav*? He would probably find the everyday demands of *Halachah* very confining. Probably, he would do best as a teacher of some kind, but where should he settle and how should he earn his living?

After much consideration, he finally raised the subject with Elya himself on a *Shabbos* afternoon when they had met over tea and cake at the house of his brother. It was already the month of *Elul*, a good time for a serious discussion.

"I want you to know, Elya," Reb Aryeh began, "that I have been in touch for many years with Reb Meir Leibush Malbim. Did you ever hear of him?"

Elya's eyes lit up.

"Yes, of course. He is *Rav* in Bucharest, in Romania. Isn't that correct?"

"That is correct," replied Reb Aryeh. "For thirty years now he has been in combat with the Reform movement, and he knew when he took the post in Bucharest that it would mean severe harassment from them. He has suffered terribly there; they have spared him nothing. The attacks have all but overwhelmed him, but he is still steadfast for the Torah."

Elya leaned forward.

"Are you saying that this has something to do with me?" he asked.

"His main task," continued Reb Aryeh, "over all this time has been producing appropriate commentaries to the Torah, refuting the Reform movement from the text itself. If you agree, I am prepared to write to him and recommend that he take you on as an assistant scholar for this work and that he should direct your energies in general towards assisting his purposes."

Elya's eyes were wide.

"But I'm not really ready for an assignment like that!" he protested.

"You are nearly ready," insisted Reb Aryeh. "If he is prepared to take you I will give you a final preparation myself and tell you everything you need to know for the job."

Elya thought the matter over. On the one hand, it was the kind of opportunity he had been waiting for. Yet on the other, he was not keen on subjecting his wife to the strain of persecution. He decided to ask the *Rav* point blank who the leaders of the Reform movement were and what could be expected from them. Reb Aryeh, however, had been watching him closely, and now he spoke up before Elya could begin.

"You are worried about your family," he said sympathetically. "Don't be concerned. You are not being asked to take a public post, and the observant community there is quite substantial."

Elya smiled shyly, but he still wanted firm information, and he asked the question that he had originally intended. Reb Aryeh acknowledged its importance, and he answered briefly and to the point.

"In the truth of *din Torah*," he said, "the Reform movement in all its forms is *apikorsus*, the breaking of the Yoke of Torah in favor of Greek philosophy and customs. However, we are not faced here with something identical to the Maccabean influence. The circumstances changed very suddenly. In this case, people were bewildered, and more often than not they had never learned the truth of Torah by the time they were presented with Reform. That itself happened two or three generations ago in Germany, at the time of the French Revolution and Napoleon, so now we have an overwhelming majority of *tinokos shenishbu* (lost children) in the populace, and it can happen that even the leaders today are not quite deliberate sinners in the true sense.

"This in fact makes our job even more difficult, because we have to love our 'enemy' while we fight him. The Reform movement is striking deep roots in the emancipated world, and it is easy for them to portray us as backward and discredited, preachers of fatalism. Their ideas are no less menacing because of the sincere element among them, and often we find ourselves facing ruthless treachery. We have a long and hard job ahead of us, with no definite end in sight. Sometimes, it is a bitter struggle, and the Name of Heaven is at risk of shame at every turn. Nevertheless, we keep up the struggle. Reb Shamshon Raphael Hirsch in Germany is a powerful voice, and much of Jewry in Eastern Europe is still Torah-true. Everyone knows that the real battle is over the future of those Jewish masses in the East, who have not yet been reached by Western ways. In Hungary, we are right on the border between East and West, and a great deal depends on what happens here."

"And the war is a war of words," commented Elya.

"Yes, and it is a war with very high stakes. Those who live in the front lines are offering their careers and their sustenance, and often there is no front and rear. If the government is swayed then it is an evil decree, *chas vechalilah,* for the whole population."

Elya thought of Menachem, and of the emotionless letters the family had been receiving. He had no way of knowing what was going on in his brother's mind or what influences were being brought to bear on him. This war, thought Elya, if it was to be a war for him, would be fought on the territory of his fondest personal attachments. He wondered if Menachem felt the same way.

He knew that Reb Aryeh was aware of the family's predicament, and now, as he looked up, he saw that awareness in the eyes of his teacher as they met his own. For many minutes, he sat there, feeling the warmth and closeness of the *Shabbos* all around him, as he weighed the different aspects of the proposition.

"And you are saying that I should take part in this?" he asked. "Do you really believe I can handle such a major task?"

"Yes, I think you would be very well suited to it. The job is hard, and there is no guarantee of success. But there are still victories to be won, and every soul redeemed from this is a tremendous *Kiddush Hashem.*"

"Very well, then," said Elya, smiling shyly. "I'll go talk to my wife."

That night, the memories of his brother rushed over him in a wave, the conversations they had had, and the different directions their lives had taken. Love the adversary? He had no alternative, nor would anyone have, once the advancing tide of progress ran over the millions of families now living their faithful lives as they had always done.

"*Ribono Shel Olam,*" he murmured to himself. "Give us the means to pass Your tests, for we are weakening day by day."

Reb Aryeh wrote his letter to the Malbim in Bucharest, while Elya discussed the future with his wife and parents. Everyone was in favor of the idea; they all agreed that Elya had the abilities, and who knew what the Almighty might require from His people in such times?

"Every Jew has a *goy* within him," Chaim told his son, "and when he sends away that *goy* and makes himself into a complete Jew, then he also takes away the actual *goyim* from approaching to cause harm. Some Jews think that the *goy* within them is in fact their true self, and so they let it rule their lives and homes, even though they know within their hearts that they are Jews and will never be anything else. So we cannot fight this battle unless we know and recognize the *goy* that is within ourselves and send him away. Elya, what a great *zchus* you will have in helping people discover their real selves!"

Elya gave deep thought to his fathers words, and they caused him to search himself profoundly. Bayla also readied herself for her entry into the wider world, confident at least that in Bucharest she would have the proper surroundings in which to live and bring up her children.

Zissie was now faced with a deep crisis because of the loss of her sheltering contemporary. She talked the matter over at length with the whole family, and it was agreed that she should stay with the Friedmans for the time being.

She was quite open on the subject of her feelings concerning Menachem. She had entertained the prospect of one or two other *shidduchim*, but the only result had been to confirm her certainty that Menachem's impression on her had been very lasting and thorough. She would even say from her own knowledge of him that she was sure he would come out well in the end, and Chaim was profoundly impressed by this, being so similar to Feige's own words when Menachem had disappeared.

Six weeks later, a letter arrived from the Malbim confirming the appointment and saying that he had asked the community to offer Elya a post as a *cheder* teacher for his personal support. By the time *Chanukah* arrived, this had been confirmed, and it was arranged that the move would be made in about nine months, when Elya had completed his intensive study with Reb Aryeh to prepare for the task.

After *Pesach* of 1868, they began all their preparations for the transfer in earnest. Elya discussed with his father how they would keep in touch with Menachem now that he was going away. The notes that arrived from Menachem showed no sign of actual distress nor of any change in circumstances, but they both knew that many things could have occurred in the meantime. Finally, they agreed that Elya should go alone to Budapest to meet his brother, to show

## ON·TWO·FRONTS

him his own progress as a married man and a *Rav* and to form a proper new relationship with whatever changes Menachem might have undergone.

# CHAPTER FIFTEEN

At this time, all across the Western world, the Reform movement was sweeping to victory. Basking in the esteem of governments, prosperous and well-connected, its leaders and its rank and file believed they were about to enter upon a new world of emancipation and freedom. As they sat in their ornate new Temples, listening to sermons of a suitably ethical tone, they felt secure in the possession of all the virtues that had ever been advertised to mankind. Soon, they were sure, they would see the fall of the corrupt and decrepit Tsarist Empire, and the Jews of Russia would be released from their grim oppression. Then, under an enlightened democratic rulership, the Jewish masses of that great country would likewise take their place in the sun.

Yet even with all their optimism they began to sense that winds

ON·TWO·FRONTS

were blowing from the East which did not carry a message of assurance for them. It even began to seem that observant Jewry still possessed highly capable leaders, who did not at all fit the stereotype of backwardness and fatalism ascribed to them. There also appeared to be many millions of householders who would go to any extreme before they would transgress the laws of the Torah, no matter what advantage they were offered.

The Reform movement had no name to give to these phenomena other than ignorant bigotry, such was the extent to which the West, with its power, had dazzled their eyes. And in their predicament of opposition they fell back on their financial resources and on their influence in high places that money had given them. For these were the balmy days of the High Victorian Era, when the world's trade revolved around the immensely wealthy British Empire with its control over the seas, favorable to Jews who served its interests. No force on earth seemed capable of disrupting the steady rise of its well-ordered democratic domination.

Elya left for Budapest without having had time to inform his brother of his arrival. He walked to the nearest station and took the train directly to the capital, pausing only to eat some food he had brought with him, before setting out for the lodging address of which the family knew.

Menachem was not there when Elya arrived, but the German landlady let him in and told him that if he cared to wait the young gentleman was due to return in an hour and a half. Elya sat down on an old sofa, and as he looked around him at the seedy surroundings, he felt a pang of apprehension. He took a *Tehillim* out of his inside pocket and began to recite.

Late in the afternoon, when he was two thirds of the way through the *sefer*, the door opened and Menachem came in. When he saw Elya a look of disbelief flitted across his face, then he smiled broadly, gave a cry of delight and ran to embrace his brother. They stood there in the middle of the room with their arms on each other's shoulders, gazing at each other's faces, with eyes which, both of them were surprised to discover, were wet with tears.

"It's been a long time, Elya," said Menachem eventually.

"Yes, it has. How are you doing?"

Menachem shrugged and forced a smile.

"It's not so bad," he said. "I get on with things. How are Mommie and Tottie?"

"They're fine. They are happy in Huszt."

Menachem dropped his arms to his sides and nodded in reply. He hardly knew where to begin with this brother who was greeting him with the confidence of a householder, the representative of a family he loved and yet could not follow. They sat down and Menachem took off his cap, and Elya was disturbed to see that his brother's head was now completely bare. He could hardly avoid letting his eyes wander to the empty spot where a *yarmulke* used to sit.

They sat quietly for a while, taking in the novelty of each other's presence, and it was Menachem who was first to break the silence.

"You're married some time now?" he asked

"Yes. It doesn't seem so long, but it is quite a while now."

"I'm sure you're a very good husband," said Menachem.

Elya smiled shyly and looked his brother in the eye.

"Bayla's expecting a baby in the winter, please G-d," he said.

Menachem grinned all over his face and wrung Elya by the hand.

"*Mazel tov! Mazel tov!* Of course, it'll be a boy!"

Elya beamed in reply.

"Well, we're not so worried about that," he said. "The next generation needs mothers too, you know!"

Uncertain of how to continue, Elya began to speak of his first few months of married life. Sitting with his head slightly tilted and a wistful smile on his face, Menachem listened as his brother grew eloquent over the difficulties and the joys. After a while, however, Menachem subsided again and seemed to be thinking about some awkward question. Then he cleared his throat.

"How's Zissie?" he asked huskily.

Elya came awake very suddenly.

"She's fine . . . she's still there," he answered, hoping he had conveyed the right degree of comfort and reassurance.

Menachem remained silent.

"Do you still think of her?" Elya asked tentatively.

"If she'd come here, I'd marry her right away," replied Menachem, with every appearance of conviction.

Elya frowned and took a deep breath before answering.

"It isn't so easy for her to do that," he stated. "And I'm sure you have some idea of why."

Menachem peered at him curiously.

"I've got a career!" he said emphatically. "I can provide for her. What is she really bothered about?"

Elya's mind went back to Huszt and to the way Zissie had developed there under his and Bayla's wing.

"She's very fond of you," he said. "More than you may realize. But she has things in mind for her life that are not found in the kind of life you are living here."

Menachem swallowed hard and stared questioningly into Elya's face. This was the comment he had been dreading and a mask seemed to come down over his expression.

"What kind of things?" he asked harshly. "Is she afraid of the big city? Does she think the whole world is to be found in Huszt?"

"No," said Elya, shaking his head firmly. "She doesn't think that, and I don't think you really believe she does either. She has a Torah content to her own mind; she understands the thoughts of *tzaddikim* and holy men, and she strives to live according to that way. She wants you to understand that, and to know what it means for yourself."

"What should it mean for me?" cried Menachem angrily, desperate at seeing his future drifting away. "I'm studying law here at the university, the law that runs this country every day of the week! I'm at the top of my class! I write articles for the papers, and I do other important work as well."

Elya felt a shiver run through him.

"What kind of work?" he asked.

"There's a man here who is a publicist for the Reform movement," Menachem replied. "I help him prepare briefs for government ministers, to put the legislation through. What's so bad about being the wife of a man like that?"

Elya's mouth opened and closed. "What's so bad . . .?"

He thought of the Malbim in Bucharest, bearing up under the onslaught of this legislation, of the children going without proper schooling because of the damage it had done. He thought about the role he had just undertaken. How did one fight a war like this, right here in the middle of one's brother's apartment? How did one save a soul from this kind of level? But it was a known question. Menachem was the subject of a divine decree; he had been taken away as a child.

"You say that you have abilities, and you are involved with highly placed people," he answered gently. "That guarantees nothing. No security, no ethics, no kindness, nothing at all. These men have enlisted you in their cause, but they do not value you as a human being, not in the ranks of government. And I can tell you that Zissie is someone who values you as a human being."

Menachem snorted angrily, rising to the counterattack.

"And what about you? What are you doing with your time?"

Elya paused. This might be something his brother had not bargained on. Slowly and carefully, sad to be explaining this at a time not of his own choosing, he told Menachem of his appointment with the Malbim. He explained to him that this was a great *Rav* who was resisting the Reform movement and that he would be going to learn how to conduct the rabbinate in the face of this challenge.

"And so," he concluded, "I had to come to see you now, before we left Huszt altogether."

Menachem sat there for a minute, breathing heavily.

"And you talk about me and my cause, when you are permitting yourself to be used?" he burst out. "And for what! This Rabbi is an apostle of backwardness, a born prisoner. He knows nothing of freedom, of light, of beauty. When will you realize that you are being deceived?" He paused before delivering the final thrust. "You are young, and he is old!"

He smirked to see his brother wince as the words struck home. Elya fought back the nausea that rose up within him and the anger that tempted him to repay the insult he had been given. Shocked at the lengths to which all this had gone, he searched for words to convey his message.

"Look, Menachem," he said. "There is something I'd like to tell you. Truth is like money. Unless it has an official stamp on it, it has no value, no matter how pretty it looks. Your associates have ideas which they print on a piece of paper, and then they try to pass it on as the truth. But they have no authority to do that. You are simply passing on forged currency. You are deceiving people all the time, and it will never make you rich."

ON·TWO·FRONTS

"I don't care!" Menachem exploded. "I'm not going to live my life in some hole in the corner. I want room to move, room to breathe! I have my friends here, and that's all I need!"

"What about Mommie and Tottie?" pleaded Elya. "You'll break everybody's hearts if you go on like this. They've lived all their lives by these ideals you say are so wrong!"

Menachem flinched as his brother went on.

"And what about Zissie? Are you going to put her in some despised category? An outworn, useless person? She's alive and well, *kein ayin hora*. She has a heart!"

Menachem did not answer. His eyes drifted to the window, and as he sat with the afternoon sun on his face, Elya saw the harsh lines of outrage on his features gradually softening.

"What are her plans?" Menachem asked, almost in a whisper, not looking at his brother.

Elya had been pushed too far. He could not hold back the rush of words to his mouth.

"You'd better give her some," he said warningly. "Or else she'll make some of her own."

Menachem turned sharply and stared at his brother.

"To blazes with you all!" he shouted. "I'm not going to be spoken to like a child!"

To Elya's consternation, he started to his feet and began to walk out of the room. As he reached the door, he turned around.

"You'd better tell her who I am and what I'm doing," he said. "Then we'll just see what she decides!"

He ran out and clattered down the stairs. Elya could have kicked himself for his carelessness.

"*Ribono Shel Olam!*" he muttered, and then he shouted after his brother, "Wait! Menachem, wait!"

Hearing a pause in the footsteps, he ran after Menachem. Out on the street, the sunshine was brilliant, and his eyes hurt him as he looked desperately around. Then he saw Menachem striding away about twenty yards down the road. He ran after him as fast as he could go, caught him by the sleeve and turned him around.

"Menachem, I'm sorry!" he panted. "I'm only human, just like you."

Menachem almost sobbed, but he gulped at the lump in his

## ON·TWO·FRONTS

throat and straightened up to face Elya. He gave a tired smile.

"It's not your fault, Elya," he said. "It's just that there are some things that are bigger than both of us. Give my love to Mommie and Tottie, and I hope that Bayla gives birth *in a gutte sha'ah*.'"

He smiled again, the same tired smile, and then he turned and walked away, into the rays of the setting sun.

# CHAPTER SIXTEEN

Elya stood for a long time looking after Menachem and even after he was out of sight, he could not move from the spot because of the confusion in his thoughts. Eventually, he trailed disconsolately away. What was he to tell his parents and Zissie? For the sake of something to occupy his mind, he took out his *Tehillim* again and continued from where he had left off. After a few chapters he felt better, and he went to find the family whose address he had been given for his few days' stay.

Before going to sleep that night, he wrote a full account of the day's events in a letter to Zissie. He wrote that if she still wanted to wait for Menachem then he would not say it was hopeless, but that if she should choose to go elsewhere he could not advise against it.

When Zissie received the letter she thought about it for an entire day and decided to wait in Huszt until *Rosh Hashanah*.

Meanwhile, Elya had a few items of business to transact in the city on behalf of his father, and he took the opportunity to meet a number of people whose counsel and company he valued.

At first, he ruled out the idea of going back to see Menachem again, because of the danger of rancor. Then at *Minchah* one day he saw a face that he recognized. It was Reb Moshe Greenfeld, Menachem's old *chavrusa* from Pressburg. He greeted him with enthusiasm, and they shook hands. Reb Moshe told Elya that he was married and was living in the town of Pressburg. He asked after Menachem, and Elya was not surprised to see his entire face change color when he heard how things were.

"What do you think we can do about it?" he asked Elya.

"I didn't think there was anything more for the time being," Elya replied. "But maybe both of us together can talk to him."

"So let's *daven Maariv*, and we'll go over," said Reb Moshe.

The stars were twinkling in the summer sky when they came to Menachem's apartment house. They climbed up the stairs and knocked on the door. Menachem opened it himself, and though he was only a little surprised to see his brother, he seemed almost alarmed at the sight of Reb Moshe. Hesitantly, he asked them in, and all three sat down on hard chairs next to the table.

"How are you, Reb Menachem?" asked Moshe.

"Thank Heaven, I have no complaints," replied Menachem breezily. "And yourself?"

"*Baruch Hashem*," said Moshe, at a loss for words.

After this, no one was able to speak at all, until the feeling of uneasiness grew to the point where it could not be ignored. It was Menachem who cleared his throat and spoke up.

"You know, Elya," he said, "I am glad you came back, because I have a piece of news for you."

The two men looked at him inquiringly, and he went on, glad to have engaged their attention.

"I am an apprentice with the law firm of Nagy and Partners," Menachem continued. "And now Mr. Karoly Nagy has asked me to go with him to Paris to assist him in an important international case. I shall be away for at least three months, and I am glad to have the chance to say goodbye to you properly."

He smiled and leaned back in his chair. The others glanced at each other for a moment, and then Elya turned quickly back to his brother.

"Er, well, yes," he stammered. "That's certainly a very big opportunity. I hope you do well. But . . . what do you know of Paris? Who will you be with there? Where will you stay?"

Menachem waved a hand airily in reply.

"Oh, I'm not worried about that," he replied. "Paris is a place to meet people." He raised an eyebrow. "I'll have a room in one of the good hotels, and that's all I need to know for now."

He appeared to consider the conversation closed. Both Elya and Reb Moshe were now completely taken aback. They had thought they would be dealing with a rootless student, but here they were facing a prestigious international lawyer. The whole process was beyond their control. Obviously, there was nothing further to question in the turn of events, only to watch, wait and pray. Elya raised his eyes to meet Menachem's.

"May the *Ribono Shel Olam* bless you and keep you," he said, and he was sure that he saw a flash of recognition on Menachem's face before the brief nod of thanks.

# CHAPTER SEVENTEEN

Five days later, Menachem walked into the office of his law principal Mr. Karoly Nagy. The principal sat at his desk, reading a file of papers, and as Menachem entered, he looked up and greeted him.

"Good morning," he said. "Take a seat, and I'll be with you in a moment."

He continued his reading, and Menachem noticed that his mouth began to tremble at the corners as he turned the pages. Once or twice, he put his hand to his mouth and coughed briefly, and then a little laugh escaped him. Finally, he cleared his throat decisively and got up, shuffling the papers together. Then he went to the door of the outer office.

"If Mr. Kallikak comes in, tell him I'll be busy all day," he called to his clerk.

ON·TWO·FRONTS

When he turned back to Menachem after shutting the outer door, his face wore a kind of grin. He raised an eyebrow ironically as he came back to his seat, and Menachem also found it hard to repress a laugh.

"Well now," said Nagy, reaching for another bulky folder on the desk beside him. "I'm sure we could all do with a little relief, couldn't we? Are you ready to go off to Paris?"

Menachem said nothing but nodded eagerly.

"You've never been there, I suppose," Nagy continued. "It's worth seeing, I can tell you. And it's always the place to have a good time. Have you read all the case papers?"

Menachem answered that he had, and Nagy began to stuff the folder into a briefcase.

"Very well, then. The train leaves at eight o'clock this evening, so I'll expect to see you at the customs post in the station half an hour before then."

"Fine," said Menachem, smiling, and they shook hands.

A few hours later, with his belongings packed, Menachem made his way to the station in a happy daze. He wondered what life might hold for him in a city where everything was new. The biggest city in Europe, where all the talented and original people came together!

Upon arriving at the station forecourt, he saw Nagy standing by his bags. The customs inspection was brief, and it was not long before they were sitting in a luxurious compartment, as the great express glided out into the countryside and gathered speed until it was thundering along.

"All at the client's expense!" Nagy remarked, gesturing with his hand at the opulent surroundings.

"Madame Villette, you mean?"

"Yes. These litigants tend to spare nothing when they might have big gains to make. You know the story. A Frenchwoman, married to a Hungarian who died and left a large estate, including property in Brazil that is insured in Paris. So she has returned to Paris from Budapest, to be ready when the French claim comes up in court."

It was almost dark as they walked along the swaying train corridor to the restaurant car where a lavish meal was awaiting them. They talked pleasantly about one thing and another, growing steadily more mellow over the coffee and liqueurs, and Menachem was in an uncommonly fine mood when they went to their berths for the night.

He woke close to dawn to find the train standing in the station at Vienna, and he dozed again as they set off once more. When he got up, they were in Germany, and he soon discovered that the constant succession of images outside the window was making him drowsy. He sat quietly in his seat through Munich and the crossing of the River Rhine. By dinnertime, he was tired, though Nagy was still alert, working on different cases in the intervals of reading a novel.

Menachem's second night of sleep was less comfortable, but when he drew the curtain in the morning he felt only joy as he looked out on the wooded and pastoral beauty of the valley of the River Marne.

They were getting closer to Paris, and he felt keen anticipation as the passengers began to bustle around and fetch their luggage. Surely this would be the place where his career would begin and where he would make his name. This was the first step in life's great journey. Then came the beginnings of the city, the quaint, huddled houses and the wide avenues. He followed Nagy to the door, bag in hand, as they drew to a halt with a screech of brakes in the smoke and clatter of the Gare de l'Est.

They stepped down with shaky legs after two days of confinement in the rocking train. Menachem gazed in wonder at the first customs men, the *douaniers* examining their luggage, with their embroidered uniforms, their small moustaches and the swords dangling at their sides. Hearing the music of the French language all around them, the arrivals hailed a horse-drawn cab. They drove along broad stately boulevards still wet with the morning dew, past one glimpse of the glittering surface of the River Seine, to turn into a perfectly straight avenue lined with colonnaded walkways and draw up beside an elegant sign that said: Tea-Restaurant, Hotel Meurice.

# CHAPTER EIGHTEEN

Nagy asked for a desk in his room, and when it arrived he began setting out his papers on top of it.

"This will be our headquarters," he said to Menachem, who was still feeling rather disoriented and was observing the preparations without comment. "Soon the client will be here herself. Here, take this file and make a condensed version of the contents. We'll be meeting the other side's lawyers later in the day."

Menachem realized that this was going to be the start of a working morning, and despite his weariness he pulled himself together and sat down to his task. Beside him was a tall window looking out on the colonnaded Rue de Rivoli, and he could see the front of the Palace of the Tuileries behind its gardens across the busy street.

The whole city is nothing but palaces, he thought. It makes one feel like a king.

He smiled to himself and got on with his work.

At about half-past eleven there was a knock on the door, and a middle aged-woman wearing a long green dress and a bonnet came in. "*Bonjour, monsieur,*" she greeted Nagy in French, but then went on to talk in Hungarian. When Nagy brought her over to introduce her to Menachem he presented her ceremoniously.

"This is my assistant, Monsieur . . . er . . . Maurice Eisenstadt," he said.

Madame Villette gave a fixed smile at the sound of the last name, but she inclined her head graciously.

"*Enchantee,*" she said.

They all sat down around the desk. Soon another woman came in, whom Madame Villette introduced to Nagy as Deszo, her sister-in-law, who had a share in the property her husband had inherited from his late father.

"It's a complicated case we have here," said Deszo to Menachem and Nagy, with a disarming wave of her hand. "It gives me quite a headache just to think about it."

"Well, that's what we're here to help you with," said Nagy.

For the rest of the morning, they discussed the final arrangements for their testimony. Then they went down to the hotel dining room for lunch. Menachem was beginning to find it more difficult than he had thought to live up to so much elegance and refinement, and as he ate the gourmet food that was put in front of him he was conscious of an aching desire for a pickled herring. But there was still the job to do, and he was pleased with the compliment Nagy had given him for his help during the meeting.

After supper that evening, with the day's work over and done, Menachem went for a stroll around the city as the dusk grew cool. There was certainly something special about the place. The very air seemed to put one into a wonderful mood, until one felt like walking along with arms akimbo, crowing at the top of one's voice like a rooster. He went along the Rue de Rivoli to the wide open square of the Place de la Concorde, and then up the Champs-Elysees. The chestnut trees were in full leaf under the moon.

The boulevard was filled with people, more than Menachem had ever seen outdoors in a city, all of them seemingly happy and laughing. It was like seeing an ideal of human self-realization before his very eyes. This must be the true, free life, he thought, to always be cheerful and at ease, in a city as beautiful as the mind of man could make it.

He made his way slowly back to the Hotel Meurice, happy with the way the first day had gone. He first went to knock on Nagy's door to pick up a few items of his own that he had left there. There was no answer to the knock, so he tried the door and found it open. Cautiously, he entered, to find the table lamp sending a faint glow over a chaotic scene of litter, spilled wine and empty bottles. He looked around with distaste, taking in the overpowering smell of stale tobacco and liquor. When he turned to the sofa he was appalled to see a motionless body, with an arm hanging limply to the floor.

Alarmed, he rushed across the room and saw that it was Nagy. He bent down over the recumbent form. At that moment Nagy opened his eyes and recognized him. Menachem drew back, not knowing what to think, while Nagy slid along the sofa until he was half sitting on the floor. His shirt was undone, and his breath reeked of alcohol.

"Monsieur Maurice!" he mumbled, slurring his words. "How kind of you to come by. Won't you join me in a glass of the wine of the country?"

Menachem gaped at him. Was this the highly reputed international lawyer to whom he was entrusting his career? He was going to have to take a drink now or face the prospect of losing his job.

But no! There had to be a better way. He edged over to a chair and sat down, smiling glassily at his boss.

"Er, well, no thank you," he said. "I've just had a couple myself."

Nagy frowned and heaved himself unsteadily into a better position.

"Whassa marrer with you?" he asked, peering at Menachem intently. "You won't have a drink with a fellow when he asks you to? Feh!"

Grumbling moodily to himself, he settled back against the sofa. He picked up a bottle that was standing upright next to him and drank from it for a few seconds. The fresh liquor apparently roused

# ON·TWO·FRONTS

him, and he leered at Menachem. As he got closer, his face creased into a snarl.

"Whaddya think life is, my boy? Play and work, work and play! Get a little fun out of it while you're here, hey? These French have got it all, right here in the bottle."

Menachem had had enough. He got up and went quickly to the window, desperate for a breath of fresh air. He was quite relieved that no sound came from behind him. He stood looking out at the street for a while, and when he turned around, he saw that Nagy was fast asleep again, snoring thickly, lying on the floor among the empty bottles. Nothing disturbed the rhythm as Menachem tiptoed past him and went out the door.

# CHAPTER NINETEEN

The party had arranged to meet at the Palais de Justice the next morning for the opening of the trial session, and Menachem was filled with misgivings over seeing Nagy again. But the lawyer was standing in the corridor, talking to the clients and the assistant from the other side. He looked a little pale in the face, perhaps, but otherwise normal. When Menachem joined them he was greeted with a businesslike "Good morning," with no hint of the previous night's encounter. Menachem took the files that were under his charge for the hearing and went to sit in his place behind the lawyers' bench as the French advocates prepared to open the pleadings.

The case was long and difficult, full of contested assertions that could only be proven by detailed examination of documents. There was no ill-will involved, only dispute over facts and instructions on two continents that had continued in complete ignorance of other aspects of the affair to the point of creating a nearly hopeless legal tangle.

The days passed with courtroom sessions in the mornings and evaluation in the afternoons. As time went on, there were more meetings with the other lawyers, since many of the disputes had no solution other than to be settled out of court. By the time evening came, Menachem was generally too tired to do more than stroll around the city or have a cup of coffee in a *bistro*. However, it was good to be working, and Nagy had complimented him several more times on his attention to detail.

A day came when a number of crucial questions were nearing resolution at the same time, and an exceptional meeting was arranged for late at night in Nagy's room at the Hotel Meurice. Deszo was staying at the Hotel Crillon on the Place de la Concorde, and Madame Villette had gone there to meet her for the walk across. They took their time, chatting as they went. They laughed merrily as they came up the wide staircase from the lobby of the Hotel Meurice and continued down the long carpeted corridor towards Nagy's room.

In the middle of their stroll, they were astonished to hear the sound of shouts coming from behind Nagy's door. They ran forward, only to be shocked to a halt by the sight of an angry Menachem backing out into the corridor, shouting and waving his fist.

"There are more things in life than being a member of your law firm!" he roared, red-faced and gesticulating.

Then he caught sight of the two women, and he rushed past them down the corridor, through the lobby and out into the dark night.

It was already autumn, and the air was cold. Menachem strode along, breathing heavily, turning over in his mind what must be happening in the hotel behind him, the questioning, the explanations, the sullying of his good name. It meant nothing to him any more. He had decided that enough was enough, and he would take a few days to think his life over before returning to hand in his resignation. Now he knew that he was his own man again. He would go no further with these people, and he would soon embrace his brother again and tell him that he had been right. True, it had been long in coming, but at least now he was sure about it.

ON·TWO·FRONTS

A light drizzle was falling as he debated with himself where to go. He had a little money, enough for three days of economical living. Without actually making a decision, he turned towards the river and crossed the bridge to the Left Bank of the Seine. Soon he was among the maze of tiny, crooked streets, filled with artists and bohemians and students from the Sorbonne, where nothing was snobbish or chic, and where no one was ever considered out of place.

He was looking for a small hostelry to stay in, and before long, he found one down a side street. He paid two nights' lodging in advance, went up the rickety stairway to his room and fell asleep in his clothes, happier than he had been in a long while. As it turned out, he stayed there for four whole days, wandering around the Latin Quarter and sitting in the cafes over a single cup, listening to conversations and debates.

There were people here from the four corners of the world. He saw Negroes for the first time, marvelling at their strangeness, as well as many South Americans and Chinese. Often, he heard Hungarian spoken, and as he relaxed from the exertion and forced postures of his time in the city, he began to rediscover his own desire for knowledge in the intellectual atmosphere around him.

Those were days of deep contentment. He lived on bread, butter and cheese, speaking to almost no one but simply finding his privacy again in the teeming life of the Quarter. He was sure he had reached a stage in his maturity where he could never go back to the half-truths of the life he had been living. He made no definite plans for the future, but he was glad to feel he could now take responsibility for whatever he might choose to do.

Thus, it was with a calm and settled mind that he walked back on the fifth day into the lobby of the Hotel Meurice. He went over to the reception desk, but to his bewilderment he saw a look of terror on the face of the clerk as he approached him. Then the clerk beckoned to two men sitting on the other side of the lobby and pointed to Menachem.

"That's him!" he cried.

The two men walked up to Menachem and grasped him by the arms.

"You are Menachem Eisenstadt?" one of them asked.

"Y-yes."

## ON·TWO·FRONTS

"You are under arrest!"
Menachem could not believe his ears.
"Why?" he heard himself say. "On what charge?"
The officer's face assumed a serious expression.
"For the murder," he intoned, "of Karoly Nagy!"

# CHAPTER TWENTY

*I*t was only half past six in the morning, but already Elya could feel the heat of the sun on his shoulders as he made his way through the streets of Bucharest towards his *minyan.* The sky above him was a bright southern blue, and he felt strange among the Latin sounds he heard all around him. But much in his surroundings was very familiar; Romania too was a country facing an uncertain future.

After centuries of being fought over by Russians and Turks, with only ten years of independence behind it, the country was barely on its feet. Part of its people were still ruled by the Russian Tsar, and only seventy miles to the south, across the River Danube now wide and slow-moving near the end of its journey, lay Bulgaria with its Sephardi Jews, under the hand of the Turkish Sultan Abdul Hamid and his Pashas.

But here on the northern bank of the river Elya was among Ashkenazim, just like in Hungary. The Yiddish language was the same, and the German influence extending throughout Central Europe, with its belief in civil emancipation as a virtue, and its unquestioning search for a technical solution to every problem, was being felt here too.

The *minyan* was in an upstairs room in a city block just outside the old quarter of the town. As Elya came in, he nodded his *gut morgen* to the half-dozen or so men who had already arrived. He received a smile from the white-bearded man who sat with his back to the east wall, the man for whose sake he had come here—Rav Meir Leibush Malbim.

While he was folding his *tallis* afterwards, he saw the Malbim beckoning to him, and he went over and shook hands. The Malbim reached over and patted him on his arm, smiling gently.

"It seems there is another Reform fight on the horizon," he said.

Elya looked back at him.

"What is it?" he asked quietly.

The Malbim patted him once more and then dropped his hand.

"Their leaders in Hungary have sent a man down for a speaking tour," he said. "His name is Gottfried, one of the biggest 'persuaders' they have. To me it is a wonder why anyone should listen to such a hack, but there is no doubt that what he lacks in humor he makes up in determination."

Elya chuckled faintly, but said nothing; he knew the Malbim was telling him this news for a direct purpose.

"What I would like," the Malbim continued, "is for you to meet him on some pretext or other and engage him in conversation, so that we can assess him as an opponent."

Elya frowned, unsure of what he was being called upon to do.

"Do you want me to disguise my identity?" he asked.

The Malbim made a dismissive gesture. "No, no, nothing like that. Even if he knows your name he will not take you seriously. He will patronize you because you are young. I am sure he will be only too ready to crow over you and boast of his movement's glory. Say that you are Hungarian too. That will be a very good way to start."

Elya reached for his *yarmulke* and settled it more firmly on his head.

"Very well," he said, "I'll do my best."

Gottfried was staying at the home of a German Jew, a railway and construction tycoon who had become one of the leaders of the Reform community in Romania. Elya sent him a letter there in the terms which the Malbim had outlined. When Gottfried received it the next day his lips pursed into a thin line as he read. Then he passed it over the coffee pot to his host, who also read it carefully and glanced up at Gottfried with a meaningful look in his eye.

"Who is this?" Gottfried asked.

"He has come here to study with Rabbi Malbim," answered the tycoon. "A young man, newly-married. Seems studious and withdrawn."

Gottfried nodded.

"And so now he wants to study me, you think?" he asked with a wry smile.

"Very probably. It might do no harm for you, however, to show him what you look like."

"Well now," said Gottfried with a gleam in his eye. "It would surely do no harm!" He looked the letter over again for a moment as he picked up his coffee.

"Eisenstadt, eh?" he murmured to himself. "Wasn't that the name of the young journalist in Budapest? And this one is from Hungary, too? No, no. Relatives as different as that? There couldn't possibly be any connection."

And so the next morning Elya had a letter from Gottfried in his hand, offering him an appointment for eleven o'clock on the following Monday. He let it dangle as he paced up and down uneasily, wondering what to do. At length he decided not to wear his good clothes for the meeting, so that Gottfried would underestimate him further.

He was not prepared, though, for the distaste with which the passersby regarded him as he walked through the wide suburban streets to the mansion of the wealthy leader. He was almost surprised to find how vulnerable he still was to being scorned, since he had become so used to the quiet respect of his *yeshivah* surroundings. He realized for the first time how difficult it was to bear disrespect from anyone, no matter how vain or ignorant they might be.

The house itself was somewhat ornate and pompous, but there

was no denying the beauty of its surroundings. A wide avenue led from the roadway up to the door, fringed with spreading trees now in the first flush of springtime green. A large pond could be seen among the lawns, sparkling in the sunshine.

Elya stood for a few moments in the peaceful garden, his thoughts in a whirl, confronted with this powerful invitation to the life of careless rapture. Then he pulled himself together and marched resolutely towards the doorway.

Gottfried was waiting for him in the study, hatless, his eyes inquisitive over a thin smile of welcome. They shook hands formally in the middle of the room, and then Gottfried stepped back a couple of paces and indicated a chair. When they were both seated he waited for Elya to speak.

"I understand you have come from Hungary," Elya began, hoping that he was not sounding too airy.

"That is so," replied Gottfried calmly.

"I am from there also," said Elya, and as he spoke the words a flood of memories suddenly gushed over him. He thought of his childhood in Grossverdan, of his parents, of Menachem facing angrily up to him in Budapest, Menachem walking alone under the trees in Huszt in the bleak days of winter. He thought of Menachem who was now in Paris with Karoly Nagy, so distant from home, in spirit as well as in body. He gulped, and looked up to see Gottfried regarding him with slightly puzzled amusement.

"Yes," said the publicist. "I remember that you mentioned it in your letter. Then surely you will know the turns which events there are taking?"

Elya fought with his emotions. This was serious business, and he must attend to it. He had to act out his role of "babe in the woods."

"Well, not quite everything," he answered shyly. "But perhaps you could tell me how it appears to you?"

Gottfried raised an eyebrow. Was there another potential recruit here? He crossed his legs in front of him and leaned his elbow on the desk.

"Well now," he said amicably. "Our movement is developing as the country itself develops. We see a confident future as the logic of events urges mankind towards rationality and away from superstition."

ON·TWO·FRONTS

"What logic is that?" asked Elya meekly.

The question was too naive. Gottfried drew himself up sharply.

"I do not think, young man, that you have come here for a philosophy seminar," he snapped. "Please tell me what it is that you really wish to know."

Elya thought quickly and decided to move to the attack. Perhaps anger would bring the man to indiscretion.

"I wish, sir, to ask on what basis you come among us here in Bucharest," he said, holding his chin up high. "We live as our fathers have taught us, and if you speak of having something else to teach us then we would like to know why."

Gottfried went stiff with rage.

"You speak of your fathers?" he said icily. "They lived in a world of reactionary monarchies where the individual's desire to think for himself was pressed out of him at birth. What great energies will be released for improvement when all of that becomes a thing of the past!"

"There is some truth in what you say," replied Elya, "but . . ."

Gottfried cut him short.

"You are isolated by underdevelopment," he insisted, his voice rising. "We represent democratic values, and you don't!"

"Why do you contend that those values represent the only truth?" Elya asked, interested to know what answer would be offered.

Gottfried dismissed the question with a wave of his hand.

"You are young," he said curtly. "You do not know what evil there is in the world. People kill and steal, they deceive and swindle. They live their days with hardly a trace of religion or kindness. Our movement can protect us Jews from all that. We are not closed off in a ghetto. We are close to those in power, and we can build a world where the right people can be sure of staying in control. You who have such love for your fellow Jew, why would you not see him well-placed in society, peacefully praying to G-d in his own way?"

"The Torah saves from all forms of wrongdoing," said Elya quietly.

Gottfried started to say something, but paused for a moment and looked Elya in the eye. Then he calmed down a little and spoke again in a more reasonable tone.

"My dear young friend," he said, smiling once again. "The

generation of today is weak and confused. The people simply do not have the strength to meet the demands of the Orthodox faith. The many things that you require from them cause them only pain. Have mercy upon them."

Elya rose to meet the challenge. He too smiled in reply.

"Is it not written," he said, "that 'the mercies of the cruel are also cruel'?"

Gottfried jumped back as if he had been stung. He sat in silence for some minutes, so that Elya could hear the birds singing out in the garden. When the publicist spoke again it was almost in a whisper.

"We shall see, young man, who wins the race, when we travel at the pace of progress, and you are still walking by the roadside."

Elya saw his chance. If he made a thrust now he could disturb the man's peace of mind for the whole of his stay in Romania.

"Eternal truth doesn't have to go by wagon," he said jauntily. "It can just as easily get on the train."

Gottfried jumped to his feet and moved towards the door, breathing heavily.

"In that case," he said, pulling on the door-handle, "I suggest that you get on the train yourself!"

Elya stepped through quickly and walked on down the hallway without turning around. He listened with satisfaction to the sound of the door slamming shut behind him.

When Elya got back to his two-room apartment he was tired. Slowly he mounted the steps, knocked on the door and opened it with his key. Bayla turned from the stove and smiled to him as he came in. From the next room he heard the shrill sound of the baby's cry.

"How's he doing?" he asked.

"Fidgety," she replied. "He was very cross this morning, but now he's settled down a bit."

He took off his hat and sat down on the chair, resting his cheek on his hand. Bayla looked over at him keenly.

"How did it go, then?" she asked him.

Elya let out a long sigh.

"He's a tough nut," he answered. "One of their leaders. The first time I've been face to face with one."

"And that was what the *Rav* wanted?" she asked.

"Well, of course." He raised his eyes despairingly. "Heaven knows how I really made out. What kind of a diplomat am I, anyway? There were good points and bad ones."

"Oh, don't worry," said Bayla. "You can't jump to conclusions after only one time. How did he seem to take it?"

"It's a funny thing." said Elya, smoothing his mustache with his fingers. "They can't seem to decide who or what we are, even face to face in conversation."

"Isn't that only natural?" Bayla observed, smiling and raising her eyebrows. "If they don't know what the Torah is, how can they possibly know what we are?"

Elya glanced at her and laughed.

"You're right again, aren't you?" he said, sitting up in his chair. "How could I ever hope to fight tough Reformers if it wasn't for you?"

Bayla's smile relaxed, and they sat together quietly for a few minutes, until suddenly the baby's cry disturbed them again. Bayla got up.

"I must pick him up or he'll fuss," she said. "Give the dinner a stir, would you?"

Elya went to the stove and poked at the contents of the saucepan for a while with a wooden spoon. It was the last day they would be eating that week's *cholent*. But there were fresh boiled potatoes to go with it, and anyway, he didn't mind. During these last few blissful months, here at the start of his purposeful life, he hadn't minded much about anything.

After they had finished their meal, a few of the younger *bachurim* began to arrive for Elya's *shiur*. They greeted each other, and sat down around the table over the volumes of *Shulchan Aruch*.

Elya began, and they listened attentively to his exposition, asking questions from time to time. It was all very reassuring after his morning's work, and as he neared the end, the two experiences began to merge in his mind, forming a whole that was greater than the sum of its parts.

When the *bachurim* left he walked over to the window and stood there, thinking about the tasks that were facing him.

The world of Torah study, he knew, was no longer uppermost in the consciousness of most Jews. Whether it was due to the emancipation or to some deeper spiritual event, he and those like him were being called upon to "sell" the values of eternity to people who had been taught to live for the moment. And as things stood, there seemed to be little chance that they would listen. So many opportunities and distractions were opening up in the world that they would simply have no time to spare. Torah had been deprived of its warm environment, because the Exile itself had turned "cold," and that meant danger for life itself, not just darkness and lack of direction.

Whom would Gottfried attract to his meetings? People who had missed out on their spiritual upbringing through adverse circumstances or inefficiency, selfish or ambitious people eager for worldly advancement, ordinary individuals looking for pleasant company with no obligations. A few would surely be sinners just like those at any other time and place, ready to grasp any opportunity to break off the yoke.

And he himself was going to have to try to convince them that there was something else in life other than what Gottfried would tell them, something that was not evident to them by itself. He grimaced involuntarily. It wasn't going to be easy, and yet in a situation where people were hanging on to the edge of life it might be his efforts that would make all the difference.

Bayla had gone downstairs to check the mailbox, leaving the door open behind her, and now she came in and closed it again. She had a letter in her hand, and she was holding it gingerly, with a doubtful look on her face.

"What's that?" he asked.

She held it out to him, and he saw the row of foreign stamps on the front.

"It's from your father," she said. "From Paris."

A chill gripped him as he put out his hand to take it. He opened it carefully and took out the single sheet. Bayla watched him as he read it, and she paled as she saw him whiten and catch his breath. He put the paper down on the table and looked for something to lean on.

"What is it?" she asked in a whisper.

He looked at her with haunted eyes.

"Menachem was arrested," he said slowly. "He's been put into prison in Paris."

"How can that be?" she gasped. "How can they do such a thing?"

Elya lowered himself into a chair. He had no reply.

"Is there anything that can be done?" she asked.

Elya shrugged despairingly.

"He's innocent," he answered. "My father will be doing whatever there is to do. I don't know. I just don't know."

For a minute his thoughts spun right out of control. He held his head in his hands, trying not to think of the dreadful possibilities that awaited a man condemned to such a fate. The fight had come home to him with a vengeance now. What did the *Ribono Shel Olam* want from him, from Menachem, from any of them? He looked up at his wife and saw her staring down at him with frightened eyes. He forced a little smile, and glanced at the clock. There were still three hours of daylight left.

"Well there's one thing we can do," he said, and he got up and went to the bookcase for the *Tehillim*. Opening the volume he muttered his brother's name and began to recite.

"Fortunate is the man who has not walked in the counsel of the wicked, nor stood on the way of the sinners, nor sat in the gathering of the mockers . . ."

Gottfried's first public meeting was held three days later, and it attracted a fair-sized audience. He lectured on the topics of modern life and democratic progress, seriously but with a kindly tone, using no harsh words about anyone. Elya had reported to the Malbim that Gottfried was a capable man, but vulnerable in many respects. They had decided to conduct their opposition to the tour by advertising his failings as those of the Reform movement itself, through printed material and meetings of their own. The Malbim had been deeply distressed to hear the news of Menachem and had undertaken to *daven* on his behalf.

Meanwhile Elya still had to be militant. He had to be the organizer of a campaign at a time when what he felt most like doing was curling up into a little ball. But he summoned up his resources and threw himself into the task. With the help of his *bachurim* and of some of the householders of the community, he drafted handbills and had them distributed at the entrances to Gottfried's meetings. All the *Rabbanim* of the city spoke out against the intruder on *Shabbos*, their efforts coordinated through Elya's intervention. Once while they were unpacking handbills from the printer he overheard one *bachur* asking another how he thought Gottfried had come to be the way he was. The other had merely shrugged and quoted, "He who spares the rod hates his son."

That had heartened Elya's faith in human nature, but for the rest it was a desperate struggle. They could hear the new message of ease finding a ready audience, offering a solution to so many pent up social and personal problems, and no one prepared to invest their integrity in truth for its own sake. It was the test of the times, growing on itself for three generations now, with all the heavenly grace of a wet snowball picking up speed as it rolled away down the mountainside.

The oppositional meetings were held, but few people attended. Those who did were mostly not from the middle ground of waverers about whose future the Malbim was so seriously concerned. A new indifference had entered Jewish life, and people seemed perfectly ready to take Gottfried at face value; Elya and his colleagues were left preaching to the converted, standing for the others solely as a testimony to the fact that not everyone was going to succumb.

The community was dividing itself, those still faithful to the Torah now fenced off in a new ghetto confinement, all the more severe because their own fellow Jews had established it. Elya pondered at length on the implications of this crucial aspect of the problem. What mentality could ever serve to reunify Jewry after such a split? How should the remaining faithful conduct themselves in order to provide those who had strayed with something to which to return to?

His spirits declined more and more as the cold weather came once again, hearing from Hungary only that Menachem was still imprisoned in Paris and awaiting trial for the murder of Karoly Nagy. He could only talk to Bayla, and her questions about Menachem and his background served to instill some small degree of confidence in him as he searched for the answers.

On one occasion she asked him, "Who is Kossuth?"

He thought for a short while before answering, and replied.

"I have never met him," he said, "but I know that he is an idealist. He is one of those *goyim* who transcend their tribal boundaries. Sometimes I have wondered whether if he knew of the Seven *Mitz-*

*vos*, or had a framework in which to keep them, he might become one of the leaders of a truly faithful non-Jewish society."

"As important as that?" asked Bayla.

"Oh yes, I think so," he replied. "The *Rabbanim* in Napoleon's time said that Napoleon might well have had royal soul, but that he was turning it to peversion. It may be that Kossuth also has a kind of royalty and is still an honest man, too."

He saw his wife looking at him with something like admiration, and quickly he gave a deprecating smile.

"But of course, I haven't met Kossuth, so I can't really say," he added.

Keeping the hope in his heart for his brother alive, he continued his studies and his activities in the city as the evenings gradually darkened and the gas light came to illuminate his path. Then almost before he realized it, *Chanukah* was upon them, and he was kindling the first light on his side table while Bayla held the baby so that he could see. Had not Reb Aryeh told him about the Maccabim and their victorious campaign? It was the coldest, darkest time of the year, and now suddenly everything was bright and warm.

The Malbim was having a *seudah* that evening for a few people who were close to him, and as Elya walked there he felt elated once more, confident over all his troubles. He would do his part, come what may. There was a mysterious element in his feelings, a conjunction of separate elements in his knowledge, as if by Divine mercy some portion of the secret of the times had been revealed to him, too pleasant to describe.

Around the Malbim's table everything was joyful and calm. They savored the blintzes together, and the Malbim spoke warmly and informally with everyone present. Then they all turned to hear him as he began to speak a word of Torah. His expression was grave, yet still untroubled, and he smiled a half-smile through his white beard.

"Though our heads be bowed down to the ground . . . ," he began, and Elya watched and listened, captivated by the words of truth he was hearing, watching the two candles flickering in their metal stand. Lights like these were still glowing all over Bucharest, in scores and hundreds of other towns throught Europe, in North Africa and Asia, even in Germany and America where they were surrounded by the *Misyavnim,* the Grecianizers celebrating the victory they thought they had won.

Elya knew that it would always be so until *Mashiach* came. Hashem had promised Aharon Hacohen that his lights would never be extinguished, however many individuals lost heart or were induced to do so, whatever struggles might be required from those who remained to keep them glowing. And a prayer came forth from Elya that his own brother might be spared to see the victory.

# CHAPTER TWENTY-ONE

*M*onths went by, and once more the sunshine of spring shone down on the city of Paris. The citizens welcomed it with a smile, happy that they would again behold that special beauty which springtime reserves for their city. But one man was seeing it with different eyes. He saw it filtering down from high skylight windows, into the courtroom where he stood ready to face his trial.

Menachem was pale from the long time in custody, separated from the outside world by the enormity of the charge that had been laid against him. His parents had come to visit him, and at least he had told them the true story and convinced them of his innocence. They had *davened* for him and told him that they would look after Zissie until it was all over, and then they had gone back to Hungary. Elya, Bayla and son were living happily in Bucharest. Only Chaim

Eisenstadt had returned to be present today for the opening of the trial of his son.

The black-robed judge was now climbing up to his seat on the wide podium, and he called the court to order with a motion of his hand.

"I am Maitre Jean Luizet," he began. "I am examining justice of the Fourth District of Paris, and in the name of Napoleon III, Emperor of the French, I hereby open the proceedings against Menachem Eisenstadt, Austro-Hungarian citizen, for the murder of Karoly Nagy. Will the defense please rise?"

Menachem watched the formalities from the dock with little feeling. He had long since decided that his fate was being settled in a higher court, and though he had heeded his father's advice to *daven* and examine his conscience, he had not been able to go far in that direction. Mostly, he was trying to maintain his faith and trust by guarding his integrity, much as he had done during those few days in the Latin Quarter when he had been able to do just as he pleased.

He sat glumly as the judge directed the police pathologist to take the stand.

"I am Doctor Alphonse Jeanneret, pathologist of the Surete Nationale," said the expert. "I testify that I examined the body of Karoly Nagy, found in the Hotel Meurice, and I found that the cause of death was strangulation, by means of a curtain cord found around the neck. By examination, I estimated the time of death to have been not more than five hours previously, in other words at about two o'clock in the morning."

"Thank you, *Monsieur le Docteur*," responded the judge.

The defense counsel said he had no questions, and Deszo was asked to take her place in evidence. She gave her answers haltingly to the sharp questions of the prosecutor, glancing nervously around her all the while.

"What was the state of relations between the defendant and the deceased?"

"They were on good professional terms, but I think the defendant, as the junior, was suffering under his boss's personality," replied Deszo uneasily.

"Why do you say that?"

"Well," she answered, "Karoly said one morning that the

defendant had insulted him when he had had a few drinks, and a day before the murder I heard an argument between them."

"What was said?" asked the prosecutor, probing for a statement.

Deszo seemed reluctant to speak.

"I was coming along the hotel corridor with Madame Villette," she said slowly, "and I heard raised voices from within the room. Then the defendant backed out in front of us, very disturbed and angry, and he shouted, 'There are more things in life than being a member of your law firm.' Then he saw us and ran away, and he was not seen again until after the murder."

"What explanation did the deceased have for this?" asked the prosecutor.

"He didn't say anything when we went in," Deszo answered. "He just waved the subject away, but he certainly seemed upset."

The judge asked the witness a question.

"Madame, I must ask you to be specific. What was the expression on the face of the defendant when he came out into the corridor?"

"He was angry," Deszo replied.

"Violently angry?"

"Yes, I would say so. He did not look at us at all, and his face was red."

"Thank you, Madame. The defense, please?"

Menachem's counsel, a portly, slow-moving man, rose from his seat and approached the witness stand.

"Tell me, Madame," he began. "Did you see any sign of physical blows on either the deceased or the defendant at the time of the argument?"

"No, *monsieur.*"

"You say that angry words were used, but that no blow was landed?"

Deszo looked uncertain as to what to reply.

"Yes, that is correct," she said.

"Then why," asked the counsel, turning suddenly to look the witness in the eye, "are you so sure that this was a quarrel bound to end in violence?"

Deszo swallowed before answering.

"I heard angry words," she said. "They were the words of a man who had been deeply insulted."

"Yet you cannot be sure of that?"

The judge held up his hand.

"Madame," he said. "The defending counsel is not asking you to predict the future. Can you testify from what you saw that this was a quarrel of violent dimensions?"

"Yes," said Deszo, reassured. "I can."

"And have you any other reason to suppose so?" asked the judge.

Deszo quivered where she sat, and Menachem thought he saw a spasm of hatred pass across her face before she spoke.

"Yes," she said. "There is." She gathered her strength, and continued. "I heard the defendant call the deceased a drunken animal!"

Menachem leaped to his feet.

"That's a lie!" he shouted. "That's a lie!"

"Order! Order!" commanded the judge. "*Monsieur*, please advise your client that he will do his case no good by these interruptions."

The counsel turned quickly back to Deszo as Menachem sank back into his chair.

"A chance remark over a drunken quarrel? You can't pretend that's a reason to kill someone."

Deszo opened her mouth to reply, but the judge silenced her.

"The evidence is not conclusive," the judge stated. "But it stands in its own right. Next witness, please."

"Call Madame Nagy!" came the voice of the usher.

Everyone watched as a tall, bony woman with a red complexion came forward. Her eyes flashed as she looked around her, and she seemed acutely embarrassed to find herself in this position. The prosecutor approached her.

"Please, Madame," he asked. "Would you tell the court what your late husband said concerning the defendant before he left Budapest?"

The red flush on Madame Nagy's cheeks deepened.

"He always said that he was a good worker," she said firmly. "And that he had a great future before him."

ON·TWO·FRONTS

"And was that all?" inquired the prosecutor.

"No," replied the witness, with a smirk. "He said that he was a cheeky little beggar and should watch his tongue if he ever wanted to get ahead in life."

This time Menachem did not leap to his feet. He heaved a sigh as the titter of amusement went around the courtroom. What was the use in taking people like this seriously? Why had he ever done so in the first place? No one could discover the truth in a maze like this. Had a human being actually said something like that about him or was this woman simply ready to punish anyone who fell into her hands? It made no difference either way.

With determination, the defense counsel tried to crossexamine Madame Nagy about her husband's opinion of Menachem, but without success. Glaring angrily, she rebutted all his questions, and by the time she had walked briskly away from the stand, he had made no dent in her position.

Now it was the turn of the defense to speak, and a Hungarian interpreter was brought in to translate Menachem's evidence for the court.

"Now, Monsieur Eisenstadt," said the advocate, smiling comfortingly at Menachem, who was feeling most unhappy in his exposed position. "Please tell the court what it was that the deceased Karoly Nagy said to you that caused the argument the lady witness saw."

Menachem took a deep breath.

"We were talking about the work in hand," he said. "He told me that he thought I was doing very well, and he said that he would offer me a partnership in his law firm on one condition."

"What condition was that?" asked the counsel.

"It was," Menachem paused and looked around the court, "that I convert to Christianity."

"Aha!" said the counsel dramatically. "And why did he insist on that?"

"He said that he himself didn't mind my religion, but that many of the clients weren't as tolerant as he was."

"I see," said the lawyer. He glanced around the room, asking with his gesture for the attention of the court. "So why were you offended by this?"

119

"Just the thought of betraying my origins for business purposes, for the satisfaction of people who didn't know me and cared nothing for how I chose to live. It was an insulting proposal."

"Insulting enough to make you shout at an employer who had just praised you and insulting enough to run away from the job for which you had come to Paris?"

"Yes."

"But not enough to make you want to kill him?"

Menachem bit off the words that rose to his lips.

"No!" he said. "I did not kill him!"

"Very good." The counsel paused, conscious that all eyes were upon him. "Now please tell us what your reaction was to this proposal?"

"At first I lost my temper," replied Menachem, more at ease now that he was telling the story. "Then I decided that I had enough with this man and this way of life that would make such conditions. It showed me how wrong I had been about a lot of things. I needed time to think. I went over to the Left Bank, and stayed there in a small hotel for four days. After gathering my thoughts, I went back to the Hotel Meurice to collect my bags and hand in my resignation."

"Do you have any proof of where you were?"

"No. I wanted privacy more than anything else, and I didn't speak to anyone who would remember me."

"Very good," said the counsel again. He turned to face the podium and struck a pleading pose. "Your Honor, my client is not a killer. He did as any honest man would have done in the circumstances. He trusts the integrity of the court to see that justice is done."

At a signal from the judge, Menachem left the stand, feeling completely drained but glad at least that he had declared himself innocent of the monstrous charge. Whatever lay behind this gross proceeding, he would never have to say that he had betrayed his own principles. Hopefully, he reminded himself that there was still one more effort to be made, still one man whose eloquence and prestige might save him from false imprisonment. He was looking forward to the next testimony.

Again, the voice of the usher was heard.

"Call Laszos Kossuth!"

# CHAPTER TWENTY-TWO

Menachem saw, out of the corner of his eye, the familiar graying figure in the frock coat step forward to the front of the court. Kossuth took the stand without a glance at Menachem, and when the counsel asked him to explain his relationship to the defendant, he spoke in perfect French in a voice that rang throughout the room.

He told of how his wife had found Menachem abandoned during the siege of Budapest over twenty years previously, how he had taken him into his own home, of the meeting with his father and the impression his character had made on him. He told of his rediscovery of Menachem as a journalist and lawyer's assistant during the last few months.

"I can attest that this man and his family are utterly honest and upright people," declared Kossuth. "They would never commit a single wrongdoing, even if no one would ever find out about it. They are part of the totally incorruptible element on which society relies for its basic sustenance, the element that is the foundation of all good order and progress. I cannot imagine in my wildest dreams that he would ever have raised his hand in violence against a fellow human being."

The judge leaned forward.

"What then brought him to this city," he asked gravely, "away from his fine and uplifting background?"

Kossuth folded his hands composedly on the ledge in front of him.

"He is young, and he has not yet found his way in life. He played at my feet for the first three years of his life." Kossuth stopped, and a note of emotion entered his voice when he continued. "And young as he was, I never saw him behave other than with gentility."

The grim features of the judge relaxed.

"Very well, Monsieur Kossuth," he said. "Your evidence will be taken into consideration."

Kossuth stepped down, and spoke for a moment with the defense lawyer. Then the counsel came over to Menachem and told him that Kossuth had said he had to return to Budapest immediately and would not be present for the end of the trial.

"He sends you his good wishes," said the counsel, "and hopes you will remain in contact with him until the issue is resolved."

The submissions were over. The court recessed for the day. They would reassemble in the morning for the judge's summing-up.

Menachem's heart still held a gleam of hope as he was led back to the cells after exchanging a nod and a smile with his father, but he knew that the weight of the evidence was against him. How did this happen? Sitting alone in the semi-darkness he tried to understand the process that had brought him to this predicament. What wrong turn had he taken that had led him into such a trap? And who indeed had killed Karoly Nagy? At the very least, he now had to face the prospect of a shattered career and of a reputation so tarnished that no worthwhile society in Europe would ever accept him. What purpose could that possibly serve? Was there another reason for all this, a deeper meaning perhaps? Still, he was young; his life was only beginning, and the mere fact of being at the center of a significant event was itself an assurance that he would never be forsaken.

At ten o'clock the next morning, he was led into court for the final session. The judge called for order and began his summation of the facts. His first speech was a clear and balanced account of the events of the evening of Menachem's flight. Then he started on his assessment of the evidence, and Menachem's eyes began to bulge in horror at what he was hearing.

"*Messieurs et mesdames,*" intoned the upholder of the law. "This case turns upon the question of what the defendant did when it was proposed to him that he should abjure the Jewish faith. It would seem to me from his appearance that he has already abjured it to a considerable extent, but nevertheless, he is asking us to believe, on the true faith of a Jew, that he felt insulted by the proposition that he should become a Christian.

"This is a demeaning statement. It shows the defendant's contempt for society, and the essentially low moral level of the background from which he springs and its devious attitudes to the Christian laws by which honest people in all lands conduct their lives. Therefore, I direct that the character evidence should not be heeded and that on the strength of the evidence of the surrounding facts, the defendant should be found guilty as charged."

Menachem turned white. He thought he was going to faint. Something sustained him though, and suddenly he understood clearly what was rotten and despicable in the society around him that could lead to such words being spoken. He could see his father's face in the gallery, a mask of despair and resignation. There was a general murmur in the courtroom, and it seemed to him as if there was a current of dissent at the harshness of the judge's language. But if so, the judge was quick to suppress it. He shouted for order and continued.

"The evidence is only circumstantial. However, I direct that the defendant be considered a threat to public safety and that he should be transported to the prison colonies in Guiana. Because of his foreign citizenship he will not be required to serve out the full life term of imprisonment, and so, I sentence him to no less than eight years of confinement."

So that was it. Strong hands seized Menachem's arms, propelling him out of the dock and down to the cells. A judge who hated the

## ON·TWO·FRONTS

Jews had been appointed over him, and he had been sentenced to labor in the jungles of South America. But even as his footsteps echoed along the dank corridors of the prison house, he felt a new strength flow into his limbs, a confidence that the suffering and the injustice were not in vain and that he would come through in the end.

# CHAPTER TWENTY-THREE

*I*n all of South America there was only one small section of land which had not been colonized by either Portugal or Spain. It was a strip of jungle on the north coast known as Guiana, a forbidding area of mangrove swamp split between the British, Dutch and French, to which African slaves had been brought in order to work the plantations of sugar cane and banana.

In 1850, slavery was abolished in the French territories, and so the Africans deserted to the jungle, where they set up their own independent villages much like those from which their ancestors had been captured. The colony needed a new labor force in order to be able to survive, and thus an idea was born in the mind of the Emperor Napoleon III which was called "one of the most generous gestures of the century." It was to close the prisons in France and send the convicts to work in a fresh and healthy climate in the sunshine, the "eternal spring" of the fertile tropics. The French government hoped that the convicts would stay behind once they had finished their sentences, and thus they would build a new life as citizens of a thriving colony, just like England had done seventy years before in Australia. Many prisoners in France even volunteered for the scheme, in order to make a new start far away from their dreary dungeons.

Soon, however, the plan began to work very badly. There was not enough work to occupy the freed convicts, and the entire penal colony failed to make any economic development. Before long, the jungle camps had gained a reputation in faraway France as a hell-hole, a place of deadly danger, disease and loneliness. Guiana inspired dread in all who heard of it. Eventually, the whole penal settlement became known by the name of a small rocky island off the coast where political prisoners were kept in strict confinement. Under that name it became a legend all over the world. Its name was Devil's Island.

Only vague rumors of this had filtered through to Menachem as he climbed up the old wooden gangplank of a transport ship in the port of Brest with the other prisoners. They were under the surveillance of guards armed with carbines, and he could see from the faces of the men around him that the moral level of the company was as low as possible. He realized that he would have to summon up all his abilities to be able to survive all the hardships that were befalling him. He resolved as a first priority that he would talk to the others as little as he could.

The ship had been adapted for the transport of convicts, and a series of improvised cages had been set up in a large steel hold at the center of the hull. Into these Menachem and the rest were herded roughly. Each man was given a cake of ship's biscuit as the dangerous-looking armed men patrolled the walkway outside the doors. During the night, the boilers of the ship were fired up, and at dawn, they set out under full steam into the open waters of the Atlantic Ocean.

Menachem had originally decided to shelter his lack of sociability and talkativeness behind his non-French origin. Once they were on their way, though, he saw something that startled him so much that he asked his neighbor what it was. The guards were going into the cages one by one, picking out prisoners and marching them away.

His fellow-prisoner was a seamy-faced habitual criminal in his mid-fifties, who cocked an eyebrow in amusement at the young fellow's ignorance.

"What?" the other man asked in mock amazement. "Didn't you hear about the latest news? There's talk of war with Prussia, so they're separating the German prisoners from the rest of us. Waited till we were at sea, too. Wouldn't like to be in their shoes if anything happens, eh? Heh, heh!"

Menachem gulped and agreed, hoping fervently that the Austro-Hungarian Empire would not be drawn into the war alongside its German neighbor.

For two weeks, the ship thrashed onward through the Atlantic gales, at first damp and cold, but soon turning broiling hot as they drew near to the tropical regions. Then the motion grew calmer and quieter, and the convicts decided that they must be close to their destination.

And so it was. Before long, they were tied up alongside a low pier, and as the prisoners were brought up on deck, Menachem could see the flat, featureless skyline of the endless jungle, dazzlingly green under the humid equatorial sky. Under the cynical stares of the guards, the unhappy convoy trooped down the gangplank once more. They were marched off, their legs still weak from confinement and seasickness, through a gate in a wooden palisade and into the prison camp itself.

As they were assigned to a dormitory with thirty other prisoners, Menachem began tearfully to assess his position. Here he was, at the end of the world, in a hopeless country, under lock and key with loathsome and dangerous men all around him. What had been his crime? Had he ever hurt anyone? Was he any worse than the millions of people now going peacefully about their business in Europe? Still, somehow he knew that everything in the world is fair and just, and he saw this instinctive realization as the only way to maintain himself in the circumstances.

He lay down on the narrow iron bedstead and tried to go to sleep. After only fifteen minutes he was awakened by a tap on his shoulder. He looked up in surprise to see a man about his own age standing beside him.

"*Alors, mon petit,*" said the newcomer in a friendly tone. "Got any tobacco?"

Menachem raised himself up on an elbow.

"And what if I did have some tobacco?" he asked defensively. "How would it help you?"

"Then I'd ask you to sell me some," replied the other. "I slipped in a little money for things like that, 'cause you know there's nothing for nothing in here."

"There's nothing for nothing anywhere," observed Menachem.

"Ah! A philosopher!" said the prisoner. "A man after my own heart!"

He sat down on Menachem's bed and introduced himself.

"I am Marcel Brecard. They caught me while I was printing a little money for myself down in Marseilles last June, so now I'm out of circulation for a little while."

Menachem sat up and stared at him as he sat calmly rolling a cigarette. Printing his own money! That sounded familiar! That was what Elya had said to him in Budapest so many months ago! That must have been the offense to bring him here, fraud and deception, stealing people's confidence in the truth. He deserved to be punished. He had helped bring about a state of loss and suffering by putting through the Reform legislation, and he had not heeded his brother's warning.

He let the breath sigh out of him gently, falling back to lie down on the bedstead to ease the turmoil that was in his mind. Here was a light at the end of the tunnel. If he repented now and endured whatever sufferings might still come upon him, he would surely see release and return to the bosom of his family. What a serious crime he must have committed! His brother had made a career out of fighting this same tendency, and he had told him nothing less than the truth.

Outside, it had begun to rain, the steady pattering of large drops on ground already moist and muddy. Soon it grew to an incessant hammering, a deluge of water that assaulted the mind and senses with its very volume. If this was to be the place for him to work out his atonement, then work it out he would. He started with a jolt as the

ON·TWO·FRONTS

loud noise from a steel triangle resounded through the room. Two guards strode in and herded the prisoners outside. There they were formed into lines and marched to the cook house.

"Tonight you eat, *mes enfants*," a guard shouted. "Tomorrow you work!"

# CHAPTER TWENTY-FOUR

At dawn the next morning, another armed detail roused the prisoners from their sleep and sent them to a breakfast of coarse corn porridge. Then they were marched out into the jungle. Soon, the going became very difficult, as the undergrowth was thick and tangled. The green canopy of jungle closed in over their heads, and Menachem felt totally isolated, swallowed-up from head to toe in vegetation. Swarms of stinging mosquitoes began to attack the fresh bodies of the new arrivals. Birds and monkeys hooted in the trees above, and once Menachem caught sight of the hanging loops of a constrictor snake. They were walking up a slight incline, and after a few hundred yards, they came to a little clearing where a few hardwood trees were growing. Here they were given axes and told to start chopping, while the guards stood watching from a few yards away with their guns ready in the crooks of their arms.

Menachem set to work on a tree with Brecard, his acquaintance of the night before, and they swung in turn, one after the other. After a few minutes, he felt a dreadful lassitude and tiredness spreading throughout his body, as the sweat flowed into his baggy prison uniform.

"You'd better not stop for too long, my friend," remarked Brecard out of the corner of his mouth. He jerked his head slightly over his left shoulder towards one of the guards. "That's Medori, one of the Corsicans. They're the mean guys around here. Got it?"

As if to emphasize his words, he sent a particularly fierce chop into the wood, and a splinter flew close by Menachem's head. Menachem likewise put an extra effort into his blow, and they went on chopping alternately for some time until the guards called for a pause. As Menachem leaned against the tree trunk he could see out over the swampy shoreline to the camp from where they had come. This was Devil's Island, the "green hell" from which men came back broken in body and in spirit. How could he avoid debility and disease in this environment? He raised his eyes to heaven, and he fumbled for the shabby work-cap for his head before reciting some lines of *Tehillim* that he still remembered.

Then came a shout from the guards, and it was back to work again, sweating fiercely as the insects buzzed and hummed and circled all around them. Now the air was becoming filled with butterflies, huge rain-forest specimens five and six inches across, colored with an incredible brilliance in crimson, violet, green and gold. Hundreds of thousands of them, filling the air as far as the eye could see. Most spectacular of all were the great morphos of luminous blue, hovering closely over the men, as if to console them in misery with their gay color and the light, angelic fluttering of their wings.

As the weeks went by, Menachem found that his body hardened to the climate and the insect pests. To his immense relief and surprise, he caught no serious illness, though he saw men go down all around him with tropical fevers aggravated by the fatigue. Someone had told him that one third of the new arrivals died, and he knew full well, without any possibility of religious doubt, that he would only survive if the Almighty had mercy upon him.

The weeks grew into months, still with no word from Europe.

There was no noticeable change in the seasons so near the Equator, always the same sultry, humid sunshine and the lunatic showers of rain. Once, the tail of a hurricane blew over the territory, leaving a trail of damage which the prisoners had to clear up. Menachem settled into a torpid routine of work and rest, seeking only to stay alive and hopeful. He never thought of Paris, and hardly even of his home in Hungary, nor did he reflect on the intellectual topics that had once been his preoccupation. He found, however, that by not doing so he was beginning to live more in a manner of acceptance than of questioning, thinking along more kindly and less disturbing lines.

It was one evening, a full year after his arrival, when the prisoners were coming in from harvesting the sugar cane that Menachem noticed a slight uneasiness in the air, a silence among the even normally sullen men. He had become acquainted with another foreign prisoner, an Italian by the name of Lecci, and he asked him what was happening. The Italian smiled ironically.

"The news just came over on the telegraph," he said. "The Prussians invaded France, and it's all up with the Empire. Napoleon III was defeated in a big battle and taken prisoner, and a Republic was proclaimed in Paris. Now the Prussians are advancing on the city."

"What's going to happen to us?" asked Menachem.

Lecci gestured over his shoulder with a thumb.

"See those guards?" he said. "Extra patrols. They're afraid of an uprising among the prisoners."

Menachem eyed him curiously but said nothing, and they went their separate ways to the evening meal. Anything could happen in a place like this, a distant colony whose central authority had just disappeared.

Walking around the compound afterwards, Menachem suddenly noticed that the men were gathering into groups of twenty or more, their faces set fast in looks of determination. The guards had seen it, too, and they came bustling in holding their weapons, shoving the prisoners out of the way,

"Move on there! Move on!"

Then out of nowhere came an ear-splitting screech from a prisoner at the other end of the block.

"Cha-arge!!"

At the signal, the men rushed the guards who had come among

them, grabbing their guns and kicking the troopers as they fell to the ground. Just as they did so a shot was fired from one of the watchtowers. It was the general alarm. Menachem stepped back a few paces to find shelter behind one of the blockhouses. He stood watching in horror as the prisoners began to assault the towers and the central guard room. Firing broke out from the guards, ragged at first, then more concerted, right into the heart of the rushing crowd. A number of men fell, and the prisoners fired back with their captured weapons, roaring in hatred and rage.

The situation was running completely out of hand. Lecci loomed up beside Menachem in the darkness.

"Better keep out of this one," he said. "The regular troops will be here soon."

As he spoke, Menachem heard a volley of orders in the black night. The military commander was turning out the garrison. As the prisoners heard it, they retreated into the shadows, gathering around the men with the captured guns. In the dimness, Menachem could see soldiers rushing out to form lines, going down on one knee with their rifles ready to shoot, while the next line stood ready behind them. Their caps were white, and he realized that they were the highly-trained troops of the French Foreign Legion, held in readiness tonight in case of serious trouble. A sword flashed in the air, and they heard an officer shout out the order to fire.

The shots crashed out all together, and more men fell writhing to the ground. The prisoners could only respond with a few shots, and the first line of soldiers stood up in relative safety to reload while the replacements came forward a pace and knelt to fire. This time a bullet passed right between Menachem and Lecci, so close that they felt the wind on their faces. They stared at each other.

"Run!" shouted Lecci.

They sprinted into the open looking for safety. Now the soldiers were marching forward with their rifles at the ready, driving the rebels up against the palisade. One of them fired on a fleeing prisoner from close range, to the accompaniment of howls of fury from the others. As the prisoner fell, Menachem saw his face. It was a young boy, only eighteen years old, his arm torn open by the bullet. If he did not receive attention he would soon bleed to death.

Menachem knelt down beside him, tearing at the already-torn

prison jacket. He made a strip of cloth, and tied it hard above the boy's elbow, stemming the flow of blood. Then he turned him on his side and stood up, hoping that his primitive efforts would be of some use.

The Legionnaires now had most of the prisoners held up against the wall, and it could not be long before the resistance collapsed altogether. Menachem shuddered as he saw them dive into the crowd, pick out a man and shoot him dead right there.

"Cease fire!" an officer bellowed, and silence fell once more.

The revolt was over.

The beaten prisoners were taken at gunpoint to the main guard room, and the camp medical staff began attending to the wounded. The medical officer came up to where Menachem was still standing. He bent down next to his patient and examined him. The boy was deathly pale. As the officer's fingers touched him, his eyes flickered open. The doctor beckoned to his orderlies.

"Put him on a stretcher and take him to the hospital," he ordered. "He's still got a chance."

Then he turned to Menachem and studied him carefully.

"You've probably saved his life," he said. "Why did you do that?"

Menachem shrugged.

"He is so young," he said.

"You are not much older yourself," observed the officer. "I'll tell the Commandant about this, and he will see that it goes well with you."

# CHAPTER TWENTY-FIVE

Halfway through the morning Menachem was called to the office of the Commandant. The small, olive-skinned Frenchman in a colonel's uniform told that he was being taken off the work detail and placed in charge of the camp clothing store. Menachem was immensely relieved at the end of his hard servitude, and in this mercy, he saw the Providence of which he had been half aware all along. The work was very easy, consisting of handing out work uniforms and keeping inventory of the stock. It was obvious that the Commandant was desperately short of staff and had had difficulty finding a prisoner who could be trusted with the job.

At first, Menachem was afraid that he might suffer from the resentment of the other prisoners, yet strangely enough this did not happen. In a way, they had never regarded him as part of their society, and now his saved life seemed to confirm their earlier view of him. They no longer honored him with their sly confidences as they had done, and mostly they seemed content to forget about him.

Everyone knew by now that he was a Jew, and in conversations it began to emerge that he had studied in a *yeshivah*. Soon, he detected in the attitudes of those around him a recognition that he should not be here in the penal colony at all.

In this way, the time slowly passed by. News came filtering in from France, and it was all of chaos and destruction. The government of the new Republic had fled from Paris. In November, the colony heard that the city itself was cut off and under siege, bombarded by heavy guns and suffering much hunger.

The camp authorities again feared for their safety, and the guard was redoubled. Menachem payed no attention to the danger, though. He was thinking of the beautiful city where he had arrived over two years previously in such youthful hope and expectation, of the graceful and assured life he had seen there with its contentment in food and wine. And now that life he had longed to join was all gone, and those same Parisians were shivering through a winter, eating dogs and cats, in fear of the Germans, while he was sitting quietly half a world away in his clothing store.

He thought about it for days on end. What were a person's plans worth in the face of what the Almighty chose to do? He could lift Paris up, and He could put it down, take a person there when it was safe and remove him before the hour of danger. Truly, He was all-merciful.

After one evening of thoughts like these, he fell asleep on his bed listening to the honking of the nightjars in the swamp outside, his stomach uneasy from a poorly prepared prison meal. His thoughts wavered as he sank more deeply into slumber, and he began to dream.

"I am in a city. The streets are empty of people. Everything is dusty and dirty, and I can feel the fear in the air. I am only a small child. I am frightened, but I am in my father's arms and I feel safe with him. We are in a building now, so surely everything will be all right. But then he leaves me for some reason, and I feel alone. Again, I am frightened, and I start to cry. I hear a sound, a whining sound, and then a terrific crash, an explosion! Chaos everywhere, people rushing around, screams, choking dust in the air! Help! Help!"

Slowly, the long-buried memories from the impact of his early childhood filtered into his mind. Once previously he realized, he had been torn away from his home, but *Hashem* had redeemed him. Perhaps this dream was a message that he would once again be redeemed.

The next morning, he was sitting at his hatchway in the clothing store when an orderly came in and curtly handed him a letter, the first since his arrival. It was from his father, and in feverish haste he tore it open and sat down to read the three Yiddish pages.

Chaim Eisenstadt was writing from Budapest. He had come there because Kossuth had formed doubts about the trial and was using his connections to have it reopened. Because of the disruption in France, though, there was nothing he could do for the time being. Zissie was with them in the city, and she shared their confidence that everything would be put to rights. Elya and Bayla were in Bucharest, *davening* for him like everyone else.

There were tears in Menachem's eyes as he folded the letter. He had often thought of how his family might be faring in his absence, but he had been too occupied with his survival to wonder what they were doing to help him. The fact that Zissie was still loyal to him was overwhelming, and he pledged to himself to do whatever was needed to be worthy of her.

There and then, he said as many chapters of *Tehillim* as he could remember. He wrote back saying that he was eagerly awaiting any help that could materialize. Struck by the coincidence between his dream and the arrival of the letter, he resolved to keep *Shabbos* as well as he could. He went to the Commandant with the request and received grudging permission. He eagerly approached the day feeling prepared for higher insights and values.

So indeed it proved. Unable to make *Kiddush* or light a candle, he sat in contemplation. Slowly, his body began to feel less confining. His mind went back to his childhood and to the time he spent in *yeshivah*. He realized that the studies and *mitzvos* of those times had made their impression on his outer shell, a shell that was now beginning to soften.

In this way, he managed to get through the weeks of the unchanging climate, talking occasionally with the others. Some of the prisoners told him their stories, and though many were ruthless criminals, there were still plenty who had tales of hardship and injustice, enough to drive them to desperation. This caused him to reflect much more deeply on the nature of wrongdoing and of justice. Why did people have to suffer? But even as he asked the question, he knew that only the future would provide the answers.

News continued to arrive of the disasters suffered by France in the war. In March they heard that the city of Paris had been taken over by Communists, in defiance of both the Germans and the French government outside the city. Murder and looting had become the rule, and people feared for their lives from the revenge of the mob.

So this is what the Emancipation can bring, thought Menachem. People are convinced there is no absolute morality, and soon the great city is being looted by the Commune for sheer love of revenge and disorder. We thought the secular world was naturally reasonable and peaceful, yet underneath it all there is enough hatred to kill out whole classes of society. They don't want an easy religion; they throw all thought of morality to the ground. What did we start? What are we caught up in? Where will it end?

He did not have an answer. He wondered what Kossuth was thinking of all this. Then he realized that Kossuth also belonged to the past and would be unable to finish what he had started. Only Hashem guides and controls.

All through the weeks of the Paris Commune, the guards in the camp didn't relax for a moment, such was their fear of the rising of the underdog. But there was no sign that the men would make plans for action as they had done before. They grew restive at the news that the French troops had re-entered the city and begun shooting the Communist leaders wherever they found them, but soon the prisoners too were looking down the barrel of a gun.

Order was restored in France. The Germans left the country, keeping two of its provinces under their occupation.

Finally, a letter came from Kossuth himself in Budapest. Menachem read it slowly and carefully, for it contained the message he had waited so long to hear.

"My dear Menachem," Kossuth wrote. "I hope this letter finds you well, as I am sure you know that the members of your family have been praying day and night for your safe deliverance. Your trial seemed strange to me at the time, all the more so when I was told what the judge had said in his summation. I was sure that proper investigation would bring true evidence to light. Now I am able to tell you that it has indeed turned out that way. Madame Nagy inherited all her husband's property after his death. She began saying in public that it was just as well, because he had been planning to divorce her and would have left her with nothing. Of course, this was suspicious, and many people, including the police, wondered whether she herself might have killed him for this reason. There was no proof of it though, so the matter rested.

"Then I heard a rumor that Madame Villette and Nagy had made a secret financial arrangement from which Villette expected to profit greatly, but the arrangement had fallen through when Nagy had been killed. I contacted Deszo here in Budapest and asked her if she knew anything about a secret agreement between Madame Villette and Nagy. She immediately flew into a rage. She assumed that I knew far more than I did, and she defended herself by denouncing Madame Villette for plotting to take away the inheritance.

"Soon, the whole truth came out. Deszo had overheard Nagy secretly plotting with Villette to handle the lawsuit in such a way as to exclude Deszo from the settlement. In return for his efforts, Nagy would get a part of the property which would have gone to Deszo. She was still wondering what to do when she saw you run out of the hotel after the argument, and she saw her chance to kill him later and put the blame on you. So it turns out that Madame Nagy was innocent after all, and Deszo was the guilty one. I had her arrested in Budapest, and the French were preparing to extradite her to Paris for trial there when the war broke out. Now the case against you has been reopened. I have secured an assurance from the French that a warrant will be sent immediately to Guiana to bring you back to Europe."

Ten days later, Menachem was called to the office of the Commandant, where a uniformed official stood to attention before him and read out the text of a document.

"By order of the Minister of Justice of the French Republic, the prisoner Menachem Eisenstadt is to be released from confinement and placed in the custody of the Governor of the Colony of Guiana prior to repatriation."

And so, with his few belongings in his hands, Menachem was escorted through the gate in the palisade under the stares of the prisoners and guards. He was taken to the Governor's palace in the town of Cayenne and given a room in a wing of the wooden building. When asked if he needed anything, he asked for kosher food or facilities to prepare it, and this he was granted.

The room was large and airy, sheltered from the sun. He felt light and free in it, because he knew what direction his life would be taking from now on.

Before long, he was on a steamer heading out of the harbor. All through his voyage in that summer of 1871, the seas were calm and blue. The wind seemed only to blow him closer to his destination.

# CHAPTER TWENTY-SIX

Menachem had to pinch himself to make sure he was not dreaming as he sat at the family table in Budapest, looking at the faces around him. That morning, he had arrived by train from Paris with his father after being discharged from custody. He had met Kossuth at the station in Budapest and thanked him for his concern. Kossuth had embraced him and kissed him, wished him well and then gone away. Now he was sitting at an early supper with his parents. Elya and Bayla were there with their baby son. Zissie, too, was sitting across the table from him, and she was smiling, because she had just accepted his marriage proposal.

The conversation was turning to the future, and Menachem asked his father where he thought he should go.

"I have been out of Europe for a long time," he said, "and

somehow I feel I couldn't live here again. So much happened in my life on wild territory that I can't see myself getting anywhere in a regular civilized country. And Europe is too turbulent now, too full of fanaticism and lies."

Chaim nodded.

"Once a person has been touched by real truth it's hard for him to live in an ordinary society," he said. He smiled gravely. "I can only see one solution."

Everyone waited to hear his suggestion.

"You should go to Eretz Yisrael," said Chaim.

Menachem looked across at Zissie, and their eyes lit up. Yes, that would be the place. The country almost empty of people, beautiful and untouched, filled with spiritual blessing to an unimaginable degree. There they could learn and follow Torah among great *tzaddikim*, away from non-Jewish company and external concerns. There they could grow up together, to be the Jews that they truly were.

Feige looked doubtful.

"There isn't much in the cupboard there," she said. "It can be a hard life."

"It can't be harder than Devil's Island," Menachem said seriously, and everyone fell silent.

"Listen to the martyr!" Zissie suddenly cried out.

Menachem had to smile as they all laughed with her.

"So it's decided," he said, and again he looked at his bride across the table.

They would live a new life together, they would be pioneers. Eretz Yisrael was "acquired through suffering," and surely there they would find the faith and truth that the Almighty had laid in store for them. Perhaps there would be other battles and other trials, but they were young yet, and their hopes were high. For them alone the world had been created.